Mary and the Duke

MARY
AND THE
DUKE

DAISY CHAPMAN

Matador
9 Priory Business Park,
Wistow Road, Kibworth Beauchamp,
Leicestershire. LE8 0RX
Tel: 0116 279 2299
Email: books@troubador.co.uk
Web: www.troubador.co.uk/matador
Twitter: @matadorbooks

ISBN 978 1 8004 6517 6

British Library Cataloguing in Publication Data.
A catalogue record for this book is available from the British Library.

Printed and bound in Great Britain by 4edge Limited
Typeset in 11pt Aldine401 BT by Troubador Publishing Ltd, Leicester, UK

Matador is an imprint of Troubador Publishing Ltd

This book is dedicated to my loved ones who are no longer here and always believed in me.

Chapter One

The village of Cattleton in the county of Derbyshire in the Midlands is the setting for our story and begins with the death of the former Duke Cravendish. He was believed to be a mad man, though that hadn't always been the case. Something had happened over the years to make Oscar Cravendish turn into a recluse who then went mad, and he ended up believing that his own household staff were out to kill or harm him. That is how he managed to meet his end, by accidentally throwing himself out of an upstairs window while trying to escape them.

However, as the aforementioned Duke Cravendish died without having any children, the title should have passed on to the next male relation but due to the fact that Duke Cravendish had drawn up a will long before he lost his mind, he had disowned his younger brother Henry and cut him out of his will, meaning the title now passed on to his oldest nephew, Dylan Cravendish.

Lady Beatrice was informed of her eldest brother's untimely death by the local doctor.

"I'm sorry for your loss, Lady Beatrice. There was nothing that could be done; he just threw himself out of an upstairs window," explained Doctor White.

Jacob Petterson, who was the family solicitor, called in as well after hearing of Oscar Cravendish's death, and the contents of Oscar's will were brought to life.

"Oscar drew up his will with me after hearing of how your late husband Lord Hunter managed to arrange his will so that you inherited everything."

"I don't understand. If Henry, my other brother, doesn't inherit the title, then who does?" asked Lady Beatrice, puzzled by the news.

"Your eldest nephew, Dylan Cravendish, is next in line."

"Do you know why Oscar cut Henry out of the title?"

"No, he never told me; he just asked me to arrange it so it would skip over his brother, though he did include some special requirements to follow on with. Now, if you could inform us on how and where to find Dylan Cravendish, Lady Beatrice."

Lady Beatrice informed Mr Petterson that Dylan wouldn't be easy to track down as he spent most of his time at sea but that he usually docked his ship at a port in Bristol, which was a starting point. So, a messenger was dispatched to Bristol to track down Dylan Cravendish and inform him of his newly inherited title.

It took nearly a week for the messenger to reach Bristol. He didn't have much to go on as Lady Beatrice didn't know what Dylan Cravendish's ship was called, but what he did know was that Dylan Cravendish was the captain of his own ship. Bristol was a city, which meant that there were a lot more taverns than the messenger was expecting there to be.

"Captain Cravendish, sir, you told me to inform you if someone ever came asking after you. Well, I saw a gentleman earlier asking after you; a messenger, by all accounts, but he's not from around these here parts. A northerner, judging by his accent," said Tommy, excited that he had news to pass on.

"Thank you, Tommy," said Captain Cravendish as he tossed the boy a few coins for his information.

"What do you think that's all about, Captain? Are we to expect trouble?" asked Skip, Captain Cravendish's second-in-command.

"I'm not sure, Skip, but best to be on our guard to be on the safe side."

The messenger must have called into half a dozen taverns before he entered the current one where the owner was able to help him.

"You're in luck. Captain Cravendish is over there in the corner," said the tavern owner.

"Thank you, kind sir," replied the messenger, who then headed off to Captain Cravendish's table. "Excuse me, sir, are you Captain Cravendish?" he asked.

"That's me. And who might you be? I've heard someone has been asking for me. I presume that is you," replied Captain Cravendish in a curious voice.

"Yes, that is me, and I need to speak to you regarding a very important matter. If we could speak privately, Captain Cravendish?"

"Right, come this way. It leads to a private room where we can talk. So, what is it that you're after me for? I can't place you. Have we ever met before?"

"No, we have not met before. However, I'm here with some grave news for you regarding your uncle Duke Cravendish of Cattleton."

"What about him? I've not seen my uncle for many years."

"I'm afraid to tell you that your uncle Oscar Cravendish has now passed on, and he has left his estate and title to you. Here's the address of Mr Petterson, your late uncle's solicitor. You will need to be there in the next ten days. The rest of the information you require is enclosed in this letter. All the best to you, Duke Cravendish. I bid you farewell," said the messenger, who then made his leave.

Then Captain Cravendish returned to his table to rejoin Skip and the rest of his crew.

"Well, what was that about, Captain? Is trouble brewing?" asked Skip with concern in his voice.

"No Skip, that was a messenger regarding my uncle Oscar Cravendish, who has recently passed on, leaving me his title and estate. I need to leave straight away to go to the village where my uncle lived: Cattleton in Derbyshire, in the Midlands. So, Skip, look after things here until I get back. Hopefully I won't be gone long," said Captain Cravendish as he gathered up his belongings and left the tavern.

In the Barker household, Mary Barker was reading the morning newspaper.

"I can't believe William and the rest of the naval unit can't do anything about this sea captain Cravendish. I'm sure a man like that has broken the law in some way, but William says they can't charge Captain Cravendish with anything without any proper proof of piracy being committed as the courts would just overrule them," said Mary.

"Well, Mary, that's just the way the law works. No evidence shows the courts no crime has been committed. One is innocent until proof can be produced to show evidence of a crime," said Mr Barker.

"So, Mary, is there any other news in the paper to share, or is it all about sea captains not being charged with any crimes they may or may not have committed?" said Mrs Barker.

"Oh yes, the reason I brought up this Captain Cravendish in the first place was because I was reading about a Duke Cravendish who has recently passed on. Apparently he owned a very large estate here in Cattleton, it says."

"Oh yes, he owned the land not far from here. I never had much to do with the man. Nor did anybody else for that matter; the poor man went raving mad unfortunately," remarked Mr Barker.

"Oh my, Mary, you may have just stumbled upon some interesting information at last. I was so worried you were only interested in the news; now I see you are interested in ballroom conversations," said Mrs Barker happily.

"Well, Mary, it appears you have met your mother's approval on this bit of information."

"Oh, Mr Barker, don't encourage her so. That would explain why the Valentines came back to Cattleton so suddenly; clearly, they heard the news of a new Duke Cravendish and hurried back to Cattleton. Obviously Helena didn't find a husband when they were in London for the winter season, and they are now hoping that Helena will land the new duke. At least your sisters showed interest in ballroom dancing and the arts. You, on the other hand, Mary, were always chasing after William, sword fighting and studying textbooks and the newspaper. And, to my disappointment, your father encouraged you to explore your interests and take part in activities not suitable for a young lady to take part in. It's no wonder you get all these ideas in your head, Mary."

"My dear, if you're quite done lecturing Mary, I have heard some news that may be of interest to you."

"Well, what is it, Mr Barker? Pray tell me at once. Clearly we get the papers here weeks later than the Londoners do," said Mrs Barker excitedly.

"I have recently heard that the newly titled Duke Cravendish has arrived in our village. A young gentleman of sound mind, by all accounts."

"Well, don't tease me, Mr Barker! Tell me everything you know about the gentleman. Is he single?" enquired Mrs Barker.

"I do believe that the new Duke Cravendish is unmarried."

"Oh, what news you have bestowed to us, Mr Barker!"

"Do you think the new duke will be present at the ball tonight?" asked Kathleen.

"Let's hope so, Kathleen! We must be prepared. Come now, dear, we need to make sure we look our best for this evening," said Mrs Barker.

"Oh Dylan, I am so pleased Mr Petterson's man about town was able to track you down, and that you came up here to see Mr Petterson," said Lady Beatrice.

"Well, it's clearly apparent that Uncle Oscar believed I

would make a good replacement for him after his passing. The least I could do is show up and hear the terms. Though I can't think why he left the title to me; I didn't know my Uncle Oscar that well. Do you have any ideas?"

"No, it was just as much of a shock for me too," exclaimed Lady Beatrice. "Well, Dylan, I hope you like the estate. The servants are well used to the overall running of the place. As Oscar, rest his soul, wasn't in the right frame of mind to manage things on his own, I know it's going to take some work to get things put to right. It'll be good to have you here, nice to have some family as company for a change. You will make sure you come and see me once you get settled in?"

"Of course, Aunt Beatrice. I look forward to it."

"Of course, I hope to see you at other social affairs that take place here in our small village. People will want to see you as you are the new Duke Cravendish."

"You're planning on keeping me busy during my time here then, Aunt Beatrice," said Dylan with a smile.

"As stipulated in Oscar's will, you will need to be a great socialite as he has only given you a year to be Duke Cravendish. Fail to find yourself a bride before this time next year and the title will pass on to your younger brother."

"I am well aware of that, Aunt Beatrice," Dylan replied.

Lady Beatrice knew even before her nephew Dylan arrived that she would have to do whatever she could to keep Dylan here, as she knew deep down in her heart that the countryside couldn't compete with the adventures a man could have on the high seas. Estate management wasn't exciting; there was no challenge in it. Lady Beatrice had known early on that Dylan loved a challenge nearly as much as he loved the ladies. She also knew she would have to find the right female, someone who could provide Dylan with a challenge, though Lady Beatrice did have an ideal young lady in mind. It was just a matter of planning.

Now Beatrice had a plan, she just needed to put it in motion. A big social event full of young ladies to rule in or out any potential suitors who she could match up with Dylan. Of course, being a titled lady with money and high social standing, she knew the right people and everybody wanted to be the first to have the new Duke Cravendish at their event. The best idea was to keep Dylan busy with social obligations and stop him thinking about what he would be missing out on at sea. Luckily, the spring season was upon them and there was no better time of year to attend social events.

Mr Parker, Lady Beatrice's groom, entered the room.

"Shall I prepare the carriage for this evening, Lady Beatrice?" asked Parker.

"No thank you, Parker, I won't be attending tonight's ball. However, Parker, you can deliver a message to the Peacocks' household staff for me," said Lady Beatrice.

Chapter Two

Balls weren't a favourite pastime for Mary, no matter how much her mother would tell her otherwise. *Nonsense, Mary, balls are a wonderful thing. No lady in her right mind should think otherwise.* Yet Mary did think otherwise, and as soon as she got a chance to slip away without anyone noticing she would be off, and the better she would feel for it. Mary would gladly settle for a library – or, even better, a music room – to slip into. One of Mary's great loves was knowledge, but nothing could compare to Marys first love, which was of music itself. Mary had an extortionate talent for playing the piano. Her talent at the piano was the most commonly known thing about her.

Tonight's ball was the annual spring ball, held at Lord and Lady Peacock's stately home. It was the start of the spring season, marking the end of the winter period, with many more balls to undoubtedly follow. The Barker family was present as well as every other family of Cattleton, clearly all there to catch a glimpse of the new Duke Cravendish.

Mary was already getting the feeling of being suffocated. Balls tended to have that effect on her.

Thankfully as the middle daughter of the Barker family nobody took much notice of what she got up to, no one would notice that she was no longer present in the ballroom apart from Mrs Barker. Her mother would notice, and the evening would end with Mary receiving a lecture from Mrs Barker on her absence and on how did she, Mary, expect to land herself a husband if she wasn't going to be in the ballroom to rejoice with any of the available gentlemen that were present?

Mary had had to endure the same lecture for the past five years, no matter how many times she herself had informed her mother that she had no desire to find a husband and that she had more worthy pursuits to concentrate on. Then Mrs Barker would say, *Mary, what has desire got to do with anything? It's a daughter's duty to find a husband, then produce offspring for the aforementioned husband. Mary, do you think I married your father due to desire? Let me tell you, I married your father because of his prospects and what they could do for me and my family.*

Mary was well acquainted with the features of the ballroom and was able to find the hallway that would lead out into freedom and Mary's safe place, also known as the Peacocks' library. The room was nicely empty as everyone else was in the ballroom. The lounger in the room was situated by the fire and was clearly waiting for her arrival. Someone had also left a copy of Mary's favourite book on the side table, along with a candle. Clearly the Peacocks' household staff had set the room up for her arrival.

Mary was so caught up in the book she was reading that she didn't detect that her secret hideaway was going to be invaded. Then, all of a sudden, the sound of giggling broke the silence in the room and somebody practically fell over the side of the lounger and fell on top of Mary.

"Oh my, I am sorry. It appears this room is already occupied," said an unknown male voice.

"Oh, I should have known it was you, Mary Barker," said Helena Valentine, annoyed by Mary's presence.

"Well, I should have known it was you, Helena Valentine. I see you're the same as you were before you went off to London for the winter season," replied Mary.

"That I am, Mary. Now, how about you leave and let us conduct our business in private? Now run along, back to the ballroom with you."

Mary was just on her way out of the library when the gentleman who had come in with Helena finally decided to speak.

"Did you say this is Miss Mary Barker?" asked the gentleman who had come in with Helena in a curious voice.

"Yes, I'm Miss Mary Barker," replied Mary, who was just as curious to find out why finding out that she was Miss Mary Barker was so interesting.

"So, you're the infamous Miss Mary Barker, the spinster daughter of the Barkers who refuses to consider marriage and would rather peruse the field of academics like a man. I can't see why you're so against marriage; it's not like you are unattractive or have no prospects to offer a potential suitor. I hear that your two older sisters, Elizabeth and Jane, have made marrying well an art form. Which has me wondering why you wouldn't want to follow in their footsteps. However, it could be down to your youngest sister, Linda. I believe she ended up trapping a man into marriage. That is, if I've got your family background correct."

"Well, it seems you've heard all about my family from the village gossips and that's how you are judging me, but I am afraid, dear sir, you have me at a disadvantage as I, for one, have no idea who you are."

"Oh Mary, come now, you must know who he is. He's the newly titled Duke Cravendish," said Helena in a smug voice.

"Duke Cravendish, may I offer my condolences to you on the loss off your uncle. I'm afraid I didn't know your uncle, and I don't think we will be seeing each other again as it appears we move in different circles, judging by the company you keep."

"You will have to forgive me, Miss Mary. I'm new to the countryside as well as to Cattleton, and I had to give up my life on the high seas to take on the title," said Duke Cravendish.

"You were in the Royal Navy then, Duke Cravendish, before the title befell to you?" asked Mary, assuming she was meeting a man who was in the same profession as her eldest brother William.

"No, I wasn't in the Royal Navy. I was my own man, captain of my own ship," replied Duke Cravendish.

"Sea captain, as in Captain Cravendish the notorious pirate, though nothing has ever been proven, that Captain Cravendish? Then yes, I have heard all about you, and your reputation as a rake and scoundrel," replied Mary.

"Well, I see that you do know of me and my past as well as I know about yours. So, are you judging me by the gossip you've read about me in the papers, rather than by getting to know me?" remarked Duke Cravendish.

"If you insist, Duke Cravendish, I can overlook your past and see you for the man who you are to be now."

"I thank you for that, Miss Mary, and I agree to do the same for you."

"Well, now that the two of you have been introduced, Mary, if you excuse us, Duke Cravendish and I were engaged in the middle of something of a private matter," said Helena.

"Miss Mary Barker, it was a pleasure meeting you. Until we meet again."

Mary could hear Helena's laughter even before she had fully left the room.

"Can you believe that Mary? She is a weird one, Dylan, not one you would want to get to know."

"Really? Well, I for one found her to be quite charming, not unattractive nor plain, not what I was expecting at all."

"You can't be serious, Dylan, to think that of her. How about we get back to where we were so you can get your mind off her? And besides, Mary would never let you do this to her, not like me."

After hearing that, Mary hurried back to the ballroom hearing Helena's words still ringing in her ears, as well as Duke Cravendish's opinions regarding her. He referred to her as charming, not unattractive and not plain, three things that Mary had never heard anyone else describe her as.

The journey home consisted of her mother and her one unmarried younger sister, Kathleen, discussing the events of the ball in full detail.

"I heard the newly titled Duke Cravendish was there and I also heard that he's single, but nobody I spoke to was able to pin him down to introduce him," said Mrs Barker, annoyed with Duke Cravendish.

"Clearly a wise man then, this new Duke Cravendish," said Mr Barker.

"Oh, Mr Barker, how can you say such a thing? I mean, really, how rude can a man be to turn up and not let himself be introduced to anyone at all?"

"Well, I must say, the new Duke Cravendish clearly has the good sense to avoid all the marriage-making mothers who are keen to thrust their single daughters upon him," remarked Mr Barker.

"My dear, how can you say such a thing when you yourself are a father of five daughters, and you still have two single daughters who are unmarried and are in need of husbands? Now, Mary, don't you go giving me that look. You know perfectly well that you need a husband and as a mother, as *your* mother, I happen to know what's best for you. As for you, my dear husband, you need to pay a visit to this new Duke Cravendish and put in a good word regarding our daughters."

Chapter Three

The next morning, Mary was out visiting an old friend of more mature years. It was an unlikely friendship, but since Mary and Lady Beatrice had first met they had bonded over many things, including their love of music for one.

"Good morning, Lady Beatrice. How are you doing this morning?" said Mary.

"Good morning, Mary. I wasn't expecting a visit from you," replied Lady Beatrice.

"I was concerned about you, Lady Beatrice, when I didn't see you at last night's ball. I thought something might be wrong?" asked Mary with some concern.

"Well, I thank you for your concern, Mary, but as you can see, I am as fit as can be. I was not feeling up to the ball last night. It doesn't hurt to miss one or two balls a season when one reaches my age, Mary. However, as you are here, would you mind playing for me? You know how much I love your playing. I'm currently waiting for my nephew to come and call on me. He's new to Cattleton and last night was his first time attending a ball here."

"You've never mentioned your nephew before. I wasn't even aware you had any family, Lady Beatrice," said Mary, surprised by the news.

"Well, at least I still have some secrets to surprise you with, Mary," replied Lady Beatrice with a smile.

"Alright, I know when not to pry. What would you like me to play for you, Lady Beatrice?"

"You choose for me, Mary."

Mary thumbed through the music sheets and chose to play a piece that Lady Beatrice had once told Mary was her favourite piece of music.

Mary was so involved in the piece of music she was playing that she didn't hear Lady Beatrice welcoming her nephew in.

"Well, it's about time you came to call on me. I've been waiting the last couple of hours for your arrival," said Lady Beatrice.

"I'm sorry, Aunt Beatrice, I guess I'm not used to the countryside's early starts. But I'm here now," replied Dylan.

"Well, your timing isn't at all that bad, Dylan. I've someone here I would like to introduce you to. It's a young friend of mine."

"That friend of yours would be the one playing the piano that I can hear right now?" asked Dylan.

Mary jumped when Lady Beatrice tapped her on the shoulder.

"I'm sorry, I didn't mean to startle you, Mary. You were so engaged in the music that you didn't hear me calling your name. I've someone here to introduce you to. It's my nephew, the one I was telling you about earlier."

Mary turned around to get a look at Lady Beatrice's nephew.

"Mary, let me introduce you to my nephew."

"Duke Cravendish is your nephew?" exclaimed Mary, in shock at the news.

"That's right, Mary, Duke Cravendish is my nephew. I take it that the two of you have been introduced already?" asked Lady Beatrice.

"Yes, Lady Beatrice. I had the pleasure of meeting Duke Cravendish at last night's ball."

"Oh, so you did manage to attend last night's ball then, Dylan."

"Yes, Duke Cravendish was there, Lady Beatrice, but I believe I was one of only a few people who had the pleasure of meeting him."

"Well, I hope, Dylan, that you came across as a gentleman?"

"Lady Beatrice, I can assure you that Duke Cravendish was a true gentleman towards me last night."

"Splendid. Now how about the two of you make a dear old lady happy by performing a duet for me? Two great talents performing together. Mary, you will play, and Dylan here is an excellent vocalist. Come on, decide what you're going to perform for me. As you know, I won't take no for an answer. I wonder what could have happened to the tea. The two of you carry on, I won't be gone for long."

"Not so subtle, is she? My aunt clearly wants us to get better acquainted."

"Well, it's lucky my mother didn't come along with me, else she would be trying to marry us."

"So, is there any favourite piece here you would like to perform together?"

"Whichever piece is the quickest to perform."

The piece of music was a well-known piece for both of them.

"I must say, Duke Cravendish, Lady Beatrice is correct. You do have a wonderful singing voice."

"I must thank my mother; she had a wonderful singing voice as well. I also spent a lot of time at sea singing with the crew, so that helps. May I ask, was that a compliment from you, Miss Mary? I must say, my Aunt Beatrice is trying to get us together and is trying to show me that you have all the makings of a future Duchess."

"Now who's complimenting who, Duke Cravendish?"

"I was talking about my aunt's thoughts, but if you want to interpret it in that way, so be it."

"Well, here's the tea. I must say, you two do sound beautiful together."

"I'm sorry, Lady Beatrice, but I must be getting going."

"Mary, wait. Is everything alright?"

"Yes, everything's alright, Lady Beatrice. I just lost track of time, that is all."

"Mary, I can see something is wrong. Was it something my nephew said? I'm sorry if it was. Please can you see to forgiving him? He's not had much experience around well-bred females."

Chapter Four

The following day a trip to town was planned as Mrs Barker could never pass up an opportunity, especially when there would be so many interesting conversations to be discovered. The gossipmongers were clearly out in full force, currently discussing the new Duke Cravendish and how nobody seemed to have met him – or know much about him, for that matter.

The current place of visitation was the dressmaker's, where Mary, Kathleen and Mrs Barker were perusing silks, cottons and various other materials.

Mrs Barker and the dressmaker were currently on the number one topic of conversation: the ball of two nights ago and the lack of a certain new Duke Cravendish. The air in the shop was beginning to get stuffy with all the people who were crowded into it. Mary was finding it hard to breathe so she excused herself, but no one seemed to notice.

Mary had just stepped outside the door, only to end up bumping into someone on the street.

"Oh my, I am sorry," they both said at the same time.

Mary looked up; out of all the gentlemen in Cattleton

she could have bumped into, why did it have to be Duke Cravendish?

"Miss Mary, what a pleasure it is bumping into you again. For two people who clearly move in different circles, we always seem to be in the same place as the other. It's as if it is fate putting us together," said Duke Cravendish.

"I don't believe in fate, Duke Cravendish. And I must say, you must be disappointed that it happened to be me who you ended up bumping into," replied Mary.

"No, not at all, Miss Mary. I couldn't think of anybody else I would like to bump into more." Then Duke Cravendish gave a bow to an unknown figure who was behind her. "Good day to you, ladies," he said.

Mary prayed it wasn't her mother behind her but clearly luck wasn't on her side that day. She turned to look, to see her mother and Kathleen exiting the dressmaker's.

"Well, hello," said Mrs Barker in a cool tone as she acknowledged the gentleman who had just bowed before her.

"Oh, please do excuse me, where are my manners? I am Duke Cravendish. Ladies, it's a pleasure to make your acquaintance."

"Duke Cravendish, did you say? Well, the pleasure is all ours. It's good to finally make your acquaintance as we missed you at the ball two nights ago," said Mrs Barker.

Mary didn't even have to look at her mother to know she was beaming from ear-to-ear at finally meeting Duke Cravendish when most of the other residents of Cattleton were still yet to meet him.

"I am Mrs Barker and these are two of my daughters, Miss Mary Barker and Miss Kathleen Barker. I have three other daughters but they are already married. I hope you are finding Cattleton to your liking, Duke Cravendish. May I ask, are you a fan of fishing at all? We have a splendid lake here in Cattleton. My husband, Mr Barker, could introduce you to the best spot."

"Thank you, Mrs Barker. I would look forward to such an activity."

"Splendid, Duke Cravendish. I will let Mr Barker know to call upon you."

"Yes, I'll look forward to such an occasion. Now, if you'll excuse me, I must be getting on."

Once Duke Cravendish had made his leave, Mrs Barker resumed her conversation.

"So that's the infamous Duke Cravendish! My, I must say he seems like a true gentleman and I had no idea he was going to be so handsome. I would say, Mary, what marvellous luck you had in bumping into the new Duke Cravendish like that. I'm sure his eyes lingered upon you, Mary. He was trying hard to avoid it, but I noticed it," said Mrs Barker, delighted to have finally met Duke Cravendish.

They finally managed to make it home from town after Mrs Barker had stopped to tell everyone they came across that they had just had the pleasure of bumping into the new Duke Cravendish. *Of course, it was our Mary here who left a lasting impression on the Duke. Have you yourself had the pleasure of making the acquaintance of the new Duke Cravendish?*

Mr Barker was the last person to hear his wife's tales of their meeting with the new Duke Cravendish.

"My, Mr Barker, we've just had the pleasure of meeting

Duke Cravendish. I took the honour of informing the Duke that you would show him the lake and the best place to fish. Please, dear husband, please make the new Duke Cravendish feel welcome here. I would hate for our girls to lose out because you haven't been to see him. Duke Cravendish came across as such a nice gentleman and he took to our Mary. He couldn't take his eyes off her. Can you imagine, Mr Barker, what it would be like to have a duke in the family?"

Mary suddenly lost her temper with her mother.

"Mother, would you stop going on about Duke Cravendish? All he did was say hello to us. I would expect him to do the same thing if we were any other family," said Mary.

"Mary, you need to be more observant of men. It wasn't just hello, there was something in his eyes that his words weren't conveying. Also, Mary, when a gentleman of good breeding takes a liking to one's daughter, one wants to let everyone know about it; it's only natural. Just you wait, Mary, until you have daughters of your own, then you will understand. Now don't go giving me any of that 'not getting married' stuff again, Mary."

"Let her be, my dear. I can't be dealing with the pair of you bickering with one another."

Later that day an invitation arrived from the Blackwood estate. Mr and Mrs Blackwood were a well-to-do couple from Cattleton. The invitation was for both the Miss Barkers to attend a dinner party that the Blackwoods were going to be holding in a couple of days' time.

"Oh, an invitation to the Blackwoods' is such an

honour. Word must have spread about how you made an impression on Duke Cravendish. What marvellous news! I've heard the Blackwoods have such impeccable taste. No doubt Duke Cravendish will be attending. Oh, Mr Barker, can you make sure Mr Wilkes has the carriage made up in tip-top condition for our girls?"

"I'm sure Mr Wilkes is more than capable of making the arrangements."

"Splendid! Well, now that's taken care of, I do believe we have other arrangements to be getting on with."

"Well, in that case, if my presence is no longer required, I shall retire to my study."

"Well, we must make sure your presence at the dinner party is well noticed, Mary. I'll make sure I pick something out for you myself. You'll need to look as good as possible."

Chapter Five

Two days later, the Barker carriage pulled up outside the Blackwoods' estate, where a servant was waiting to help them out of the carriage and another servant was at the doorway to lead them into the ballroom, introducing Miss Mary Barker and Miss Kathleen Barker.

Mrs Blackwood came across to escort them down.

"Ladies, I'm pleased you were both able to make it. I've heard you've had the honour of meeting our guest of honour Duke Cravendish, but you won't have met his companion Lord Bloom; he only just arrived in Cattleton yesterday. Come, let me introduce you both," said Mrs Blackwood.

"Duke Cravendish, Lord Bloom, may I introduce you both to the Barker sisters, Miss Mary and Miss Kathleen," said Mrs Blackwood.

"Ladies, it's a pleasure to meet you both again. Let me introduce you to my dearest and closest friend, Lord Bloom," said Duke Cravendish.

"Ladies, it is a pleasure to make your acquaintance," said Lord Bloom.

"Lord Bloom here is kindly helping me to get my late uncle's estate in order."

"What Duke Cravendish is saying is that my background is in estate management, so I was the ideal person to assist."

"That is very good of you, Lord Bloom. Duke Cravendish is lucky to have such a good friend in you," said Mary.

"Not at all; I am the lucky one. I've always wanted to visit this part of the country but never had the opportunity to come before, so when I received the invitation to come to Cattleton, I was like an excited schoolboy looking forward to a new adventure," explained Lord Bloom.

"Have you had the pleasure of meeting many of the residents of Cattleton yet, Lord Bloom?" asked Kathleen.

"No, not as yet, this is my first outing. Dylan says he's not seen many of the residents of Cattleton yet either," replied Lord Bloom.

"It's a shame the Valentines are not here as I believe Duke Cravendish has met them, at least."

"Yes, quite right you are, Miss Mary."

"Ladies and gentlemen, dinner is now being served in the dining room," said Clifford, the butler.

"If you all wouldn't mind escorting your partners through to the dining hall," said Mrs Blackwood. She was making sure all the ladies present had a gentleman to escort them in.

"Duke Cravendish, would you escort Miss Mary Barker? And Lord Bloom, would you escort Miss Kathleen Barker?"

The dinner was served in such a sophisticated style even the conversation was being arranged by Mrs Blackwood so whenever the conversation was on its final outing Mrs

Blackwood would be on hand to intervene with a new topic of conversation.

After the dinner was served, Mrs Blackwood asked Mary if she would come and play for them.

"Mary is a truly talented artist on the piano. Do you enjoy the pleasure of music yourself, Duke Cravendish?"

"I can think of no better way to finish off such a delightful evening, Mrs Blackwood."

"Splendid that you are in agreement with us."

Mary approached the piano, taking her seat on the bench in front of it. She turned the pages of the music book until she came across the exact piece she wished to play for them. While other members of the party followed Mr and Mrs Blackwood's advice and took to the sofas, Duke Cravendish took the position of standing by the piano.

"I find it amazing, Miss Mary, that you would choose to play another favourite piece of mine. Can you imagine what other things we may like that we could share?"

Mary felt herself stumble over a wrong note while she was taking in what Duke Cravendish had just said. No one seemed to notice though.

"Duke Cravendish, would you like to take a seat?" asked Mrs Blackwood.

"If it doesn't offend you, Mrs Blackwood, I would very much enjoy it if you would allow me to accompany Miss Mary in this piece of music."

"Oh my, Duke Cravendish, I never knew you played," said Mrs Blackwood.

"Well, I'm not a talented player like Miss Mary here; I'm more of a singer than a pianist."

"My, it would be marvellous to hear the two of you performing together. Music and singing, there is no better entertainment to be had. Your aunt certainly kept that little secret to herself. Lady Beatrice was the one to first introduce me to Miss Mary's talents on the piano and to your arrival here in Cattleton," said Mrs Blackwood.

"Duke Cravendish, may I enquire why you offered to perform with me when you could easily be seated next to any suitable young lady of your choosing?" asked Mary.

"One could, but one also knows that news of this evening will reach my aunt's ears, and I for one know how delighted she will be when she hears that we performed together again, that is all. You presumed I had other motives behind choosing to perform with you?" replied Duke Cravendish.

After a slightly uncomfortable start they were soon both lost in the music until they were interrupted by clapping as they came to the end of the performance.

"Well, I must say, that was just a marvellous performance by the two of you. I'm not as in tune with music as my wife but that was just splendid and I'm sure we would all love to hear a follow-up performance. Maybe you and Miss Mary here could find something else to perform for us, Duke Cravendish?" asked Mr Blackwood.

"It would be a great honour to do so."

"Miss Mary would you like to choose the next piece?"

"Thank you I would like that very much."

"How splendid of you both."

"I must say Miss Mary you may object to me performing with you but nevertheless, your body language gives away how you really feel about me performing with you."

"And what, pray tell, is it you think my body language is saying?"

"That you would rather be up here alone than with me, even though you secretly enjoy the way we perform together."

"Bravo! Good show you both put on for all of us. The two of you should perform together again," said Mrs Blackwood after the performance had finished.

"Thank you, Mr Blackwood, Mrs Blackwood. Thank you for having us as your guests this evening; however, it's getting late and Kathleen and myself must be going," said Mary.

"Oh, that is such a shame. I'll get a servant to make sure your carriage is pulled around the front."

After Mary and Kathleen had left, Mrs Blackwood returned her attentions back to Duke Cravendish.

"Oh, Duke Cravendish, we hope you enjoy yourself here in the countryside," said Mrs Blackwood.

"I am more used to being at sea than I am on land however I look forward to exploring all that Cattleton has to offer."

"Well, Lady Beatrice may have mentioned that you have reservations about your time here. I'm sure we can show you that the country does have some interesting things going on that a big city can't show or offer you."

"Well, who would have thought that Duke Cravendish would have such a great singing voice? And he volunteered to perform with Miss Mary Barker without me prompting him. Duke Cravendish and Miss Mary seemed to complement each other splendidly. Quite an entertaining evening all round, wouldn't you agree, Mr Blackwood? I must inform Mrs Barker about how successfully tonight went. I will start composing a letter to her now."

"I'm sure Mrs Barker will be pleased with your match-making skills, especially if they should lead into something more."

"I will be keeping my eyes on the situation and I will help things along if I need to. Just think what it will do for Cattleton to have a happily married duke and duchess in residence."

"It will hopefully bring a new light to Cattleton and help it prosper."

"Mr Blackwood, I will expect you to get to know our new Duke Cravendish. Find out more about his background and try to find out what other hidden talents the gentleman possesses."

Chapter Six

The following morning at the Barker household Mr and Mrs Barker are sat around the breakfast table when a maid walks in carrying a letter.

"A letter for you, ma'am. It came from a messenger up at the Blackwood estate."

"Yes, thank you for that. You may carry on as you were."

My dear Mrs Barker,

I know we have never been formally introduced but I feel I must write to you and inform you that your assumptions of Duke Cravendish and your eldest unmarried daughter Mary appear to be correct. I for one was intrigued in the new Duke Cravendish, so I took time to observe the interaction between the two of them before dinner and again after dinner, when Miss Mary performed for us and Duke Cravendish performed alongside her on vocals. They performed together beautifully. Of course, you will have already known of Miss Mary's talents, being her mother; however, what none of us knew at the time was that Duke Cravendish has a fine vocal tone. Clearly the new Duke Cravendish is a man of hidden talents, and he clearly shares Miss Mary's love of music.

From Mrs Agatha Blackwood

"Oh, what wonderful news, don't you think so, Mr Barker?" said Mrs Barker cheerfully.

"Clearly this Duke Cravendish has no idea what he's let himself in for, the poor fellow," said Mr Barker.

"Oh, Mr Barker, how can you say that? I, on the other hand, am taking it as a sign that this new Duke Cravendish is a perfect match for our Mary. To have someone who shares her passion for music is perfect."

"Good morning, Mama, Papa," said Kathleen as she entered the room.

"Good morning, Father, good morning, Mother," said Mary as she to, entered the room.

"Morning, Kathleen; morning, Mary," said Mr Barker.

"Mary, my dear, will you partake in the playing of the piano before breakfast?" asked Mrs Barker.

"Really, Mother? You usually don't like me practising so early in the morning, and never before breakfast."

"Nonsense, Mary. Whenever have I said that to you?" exclaimed Mrs Barker.

"Nearly every morning when Mary approaches the piano, Mama," said Kathleen.

"Yes, well, thank you, Kathleen. However, I have always said that a talent needs proper nurturing to grow; and besides, you will want to be ready for this evening's ball, where I'm sure you will be eager to play and you will want to put on a good performance for everybody."

"Clearly someone has sent word around already about the events of last night's dinner party," said Mary.

"Yes, Mrs Blackwood herself has written to me informing me of last night's events. Mary, I must say, you clearly won Mrs Blackwood over; she was very complimentary of your performance last night after dinner. Were you going to mention performing with Duke Cravendish last night to me or your father?" enquired Mrs Barker.

"I was going to leave that to Kathleen to fill you in. Kathleen didn't miss out either, Mother. Duke Cravendish brought a companion with him, a Lord Bloom, I believe. He spent most of the evening in Kathleen's company," replied Mary.

"Oh my, a successful night for both of my girls then. I must write a thank you letter to Mrs Blackwood for your invitation to the dinner party. What a great evening you both had, won't you agree, Mr Barker?" said Mrs Barker, delighted by the news she had just heard.

"Yes, wonderful news, my dear. It appears you have acquired a remarkable new acquaintance."

Tonight's ball had been arranged and put together by none other than Lady Beatrice herself as a way for her to introduce her nephew Duke Cravendish to the rest of the community of Cattleton – and for Lady Beatrice to get a more in-depth understanding of Miss Mary and Duke Cravendish as she hadn't had much time previously to observe them together. Of course, she had heard from Mrs Blackwood and had got positive feedback regarding the dinner party, but she wanted to see it for herself instead.

Of course, Mrs Barker knew from conversations that Lady Beatrice was Duke Cravendish's aunt and it would be impossible for Duke Cravendish not to be in attendance. Mrs Barker examined the gowns of both her daughters. Mary was dressed in her usual style: a long buttoned-up dress.

"Mary, you can't go out dressed like that. What impression is that going to have on Duke Cravendish? Go and change into something more colourful. I know just the dress; Elizabeth had it sent over last week for you. A lovely blue gown. Yes, it will bring out the colour of your eyes. My Elizabeth always did have a way with picking out colours and gowns. A truly remarkable talent to possess."

They were greeted at the ball by Lady Beatrice herself, as well as Duke Cravendish and Lord Bloom.

"Welcome to you, Mr and Mrs Barker. Allow me to introduce you to my nephew, Duke Cravendish, and his good friend, Lord Bloom."

"It's a pleasure to meet you again, Duke Cravendish, and it's nice to meet you, Lord Bloom," said Mrs Barker.

"It's a pleasure to meet you too, Mr Barker, Mrs Barker. I look forward to meeting all the residents of Cattleton here tonight," said Duke Cravendish.

"Well, I'm sure you will do so," replied Lady Beatrice.

"You're expecting the whole village to be in attendance then, Lady Beatrice?" asked Mrs Barker.

"Indeed, I expect everyone will want to be here to meet my nephew," replied Lady Beatrice.

"Well, Duke Cravendish, we will look forward to seeing you on the dancefloor tonight, I hope," asked Mrs Barker.

"Indeed you will, Mrs Barker, and I was hoping Miss Mary will do me the honour of having the first dance?" said Duke Cravendish.

"Oh, I am sure Mary would be delighted to share the first dance with you, Duke Cravendish. Wouldn't you, Mary?" said Mrs Barker, excited that Duke Cravendish had chosen Mary as his first dance partner of the evening.

"I would like that very much, Duke Cravendish, thank you," answered Mary.

"And Miss Kathleen, will you do me the honour of having the first dance of the evening with me?" asked Lord Bloom.

"Oh, Lord Bloom, I would be most delighted to share the first dance with you, very much so," replied Kathleen.

While Mary and Duke Cravendish are on the dance floor dancing together Mary takes the opportunity to question Duke Cravendish's motives.

"May I ask you a question, Duke Cravendish?"

"If I say no you will still ask the question anyway, so go ahead."

"Can I ask you what you think you are playing at?"

"I'm not playing at anything. I thought I was dancing – I'm not a skilled dancer, but I did think it was obvious what I was doing."

"No, what I mean is, what were you doing asking me to honour you with the first dance of the evening?"

"Well, Miss Mary, I thought that would be obvious. I

wanted to dance with you and I knew if I didn't ask you straight away, I wouldn't be able to find you later on to ask you, and I thought if I asked you in front of my aunt and your mother you would be unable to say no. Though I must say, you do look lovely this evening. Blue is clearly your colour."

"Thank you, Duke Cravendish, but your compliments are wasted on me."

"Forgive me, Miss Mary, I was merely stating a fact. Also, as we are already acquainted, it seemed a wise question to ask. Or was I mistaken in thinking we were acquainted? That's the reason I asked you in the first place."

"We are. However, Duke Cravendish, you are as acquainted with my sister as you are with me, so why didn't you ask Kathleen to have the first dance with you? I'm sure Kathleen would have got more enjoyment out of dancing with you than I do."

"If I had asked Kathleen, I would have deprived my dearest friend of the honour of dancing with his desired partner."

"So, are you trying to tell me, Duke Cravendish, that you are not acquainted with any of the other young ladies here this evening? Because, let me remind you, when we first met, you and Helena Valentine seemed to be well acquainted."

"Yes, that is true. However, it meets my aunt's approval to ask you."

"Well, if that is the case, Duke Cravendish, you must allow me to introduce you to the most perfect dance partners for you."

"Do you hate being in my presence that much then, Miss Mary?"

"I am not a dancer, Duke Cravendish, and if you're going to impress your aunt, she will want to see you dancing with as many different partners as possible."

"Judging by your mother's reaction, she sees us dancing together as a plus."

"I'm sure it's more to do with you being a single gentleman than with any other reason. Now, is this dance nearly over? Because I would really like to get to introducing you to the single ladies of Cattleton who would love to dance with a duke."

"I'm sure you are scanning the ballroom now looking for the perfect female to introduce me to."

"No, I know just who to introduce you to first."

The music finally ended and Mary made her way off the dance floor as quickly as was possible without causing a scene.

"Maria Marshall, how are you? Have you been introduced to the new Duke Cravendish yet? He was just asking me to introduce you to him."

"Duke Cravendish, it's nice to finally meet you," said Maria Marshall.

"Maria, do you have a partner for the next dance?"

"No I don't," replied Maria.

"Splendid – Duke Cravendish here was just wondering who he would dance with next and it looks like I've solved his problem for him. There you go, Duke Cravendish. Miss Marshall here will make an excellent dance partner for you. I believe the next dance is just about to begin."

"Miss Mary, I believe we haven't finished our conversation."

"It can wait, Duke Cravendish. I believe Miss Marshall is waiting for you to lead her to the dance floor. Good evening, Duke Cravendish."

And with that, Mary walked off.

Later that evening, after being introduced to every single female of good breeding at the ball and being obliged to dance with at least half of them, Duke Cravendish managed to catch up with Mary and talk to her again.

"Miss Mary, I believe you have introduced me to all the young ladies that are here tonight. I believe another dance is in order."

"Well, that's splendid to hear, Duke Cravendish because I believe you have not yet had the honour of dancing with Kathleen yet this evening."

"I was intending on asking you again."

"Oh well, that is a shame, but I would hate to disappoint my next dance partner. Lord Bloom, shall we take our turn together on the dance floor? I don't believe we've had the pleasure of having a dance together yet."

"Miss Kathleen, has Miss Mary always been so forceful in introducing new people in Cattleton?"

"No, tonight's different. Usually Mary's as quiet as a church mouse."

"Clearly being around me has affected her in some way."

"I hope Mary hasn't offended you in any way, Duke Cravendish."

"No, not at all, Miss Kathleen. I'm not easily offended."

"I take it you weren't interested in dancing with Duke Cravendish again then, Miss Mary?" asked Lord Bloom as he joins Mary on the dance floor.

"I am sorry if I caught you off guard, Lord Bloom."

"No, not at all. I was hoping you would allow me to have a dance with you."

"I see you have been enjoying Kathleen's company tonight."

"Yes, we have figured out we have a lot of shared interests. I hope to be able to see more of Kathleen during my time here in Cattleton."

Once the dancing was over and before Miss Mary could get away, Duke Cravendish caught up with her and steered her into a private part of the room.

"I must say, Duke Cravendish, you have put on a good show tonight for your aunt. Lady Beatrice has clearly been busy putting this ball together in your name."

"I could say the same about you, Miss Mary."

"I don't know what you're talking about, Duke Cravendish."

"What I mean, Miss Mary, is that you've introduced me to all the young single ladies here tonight. Have they all just come out of the school room? Because all they seemed to do was smile at me sweetly and agree with everything I was saying."

"Well, that's probably due to the fact that most of the young ladies here tonight have never met a titled gentleman before; you probably made them nervous. We country ladies are more reserved than the city ladies who you are more acquainted with."

"That's very strange, because when we first met, you were nothing like that. If I remember correctly, you were very forceful in your words."

"Well, if I'm remembering correctly, it was because you crashed into my secret hiding place. And I wasn't trying to, and never will try to, win your affections. As you are aware, I'm not interested in finding a future husband and I have no intentions of becoming somebody's wife, so I suggest you turn your attentions elsewhere. Good day to you, Duke Cravendish," said Mary.

After the most recent dance had finished Lady Beatrice was getting everyone to take a seat as she wanted everyone to hear Miss Mary play.

"Oh, there you are, Miss Mary. Lady Beatrice has been looking for you. She wishes for you to perform for her as you did at Mrs Blackwood's dinner party. The piano has been set up already for you," said Mrs Hunt.

"If you'll excuse me, I would hate to disappoint our hostess," said Mary as she turned and walked away.

"By all means, don't let me stop you from performing," said Duke Cravendish, replying to Mary's retreating back.

Mary made her way over to the piano but Lady Beatrice wasn't in sight as she had spotted Dylan standing at the back of the room and was making her way over to him.

"Dylan, won't you join Mary? I've heard from Mrs Blackwood how the two of you performed together and I thought it would be a nice end to the evening," said Lady Beatrice.

"Anything for you, Aunt Beatrice."

Chapter Seven

Another carriage journey home and another conversation about Duke Cravendish ensued.

"What a wonderful evening it was! Duke Cravendish even asked Mary for the first dance and they were also seen later in the evening in deep conversation," said Mrs Barker delightedly.

"Yes, we were all there, my dear," replied Mr Barker.

"All I'm saying is I am proud of you, Mary. You made all the right moves, so to speak. You will win over Duke Cravendish before too long. Also, his companion Lord Bloom is single and he's clearly a fan of dancing as well. Lord Bloom danced at least three dances with Kathleen, and even once with Mary. Oh, Mr Barker, I can just see it now: a duke and a lord in the family."

"Well, it looks like you will be having a busy spring season ahead of you then, my dear."

"Are you alright, Kathleen? You were strangely quiet on the journey home, which is unlike you," Mary asked when they were finally alone in their room.

"Oh, Mary, how can you be sure that Lord Bloom

actually likes me so? I mean, we may have shared a total of three dances together but that could be because Lord Bloom is just one of those gentlemen who hates to disappoint, and he's a gentleman who wouldn't let himself see a lady without a partner. Oh, Mary, I wish I had your confidence on such matters."

"Kathleen, how can you doubt Lord Bloom's affections for you? The gentleman couldn't keep his eyes from drifting over to you all evening. Trust me, Kathleen, I observed you two together. It's clear he likes you as much as you like him; he even implied as much to me during our dance together."

"Enough about me, Mary. What about you and Duke Cravendish? I witnessed the two of you together. I've never seen you interact with a gentleman so well before. You've clearly piqued his interest."

"Kathleen, dear sister, I wouldn't refer to Duke Cravendish as a gentleman. He's a rake, and the worst kind of rake that there is. Furthermore, if I was ever contemplating marriage, Duke Cravendish would be the last man I would consider marrying."

"Mary, how can you say such things about Duke Cravendish? He came across to me as a perfect gentleman. And are you not the one who always tells us you can't judge a book by its cover? Whatever did poor Duke Cravendish do at your first meeting to offend you so, Mary?"

"I can't tell you, Kathleen. I would hate to crush some of the opinion that you have about Duke Cravendish."

"My Lady, is everything alright?" asked Parker.

"It couldn't be better, Parker," replied Lady Beatrice.

First of all, Dylan had danced with Mary, then she had heard they were seen secretly conversing with each other privately, and then she had got them to perform together at the end of the night. Though getting the two of them together in the same room was the easy part; the hard part would be getting the two of them to realise they were perfect for each other.

"Can I tempt you to a drop of liquor, Hugh?" asked Dylan. "I for one could do with one."

"I didn't think the evening went that badly, so what's tempting you to drink? From what I saw, you were a true gentleman tonight, Dylan, dancing with all the young ladies that were there."

"Yes, that's true, I was a gentleman. And yet she treats me as if I'm the devil incarnate."

"Hence the reason for the drink. I take it you're referring to a certain lady whose name is Miss Mary Barker."

"There's just something about her, Hugh. Ever since our first encounter, there was something between us."

"Yes, I couldn't help but pick up on the tension between the two of you. Though I don't think she holds you in such high regard."

"Do you know that when we first encountered each other, she referred to me as a scoundrel and a rake? I mean, they're not the typical words one expects to hear from a well-brought-up young lady."

"Were you partaking of a particular pursuit to lead Miss Mary to refer to you as such?"

"That's not important. The fact that she even called me that in polite conversation is."

"Well, Dylan, maybe your history with the ladies is known to Miss Mary. I do believe a lot of people would refer to you in much the same way, but may not do so in person. So, did you find it offensive that Miss Mary referred to you as a rake, or is it because the young lady has got under your skin?"

"What utter nonsense you speak, Hugh."

"You don't believe that there's a lady out there who could get under your skin then, Dylan?"

"I wish you'd drop this conversation, Hugh."

"Well, you're the one who brought up the topic in the first place, Dylan."

"However, Hugh, I do require your assistance in dealing with Mr Barker tomorrow when we pay a visit to the Barkers' residence. I've heard Mr Barker's the man I need to speak to; he's apparently very knowledgeable about the local area, very hands-on. He has knowledge of the Cravendish estate but I think he will only help someone if he trusts them. That's where you will come in. Hugh, you are seen as a good man, a man of honour, and could easily win over Mr Barker's trust."

"You doubt your own ability to win the gentleman over, then?"

"Let's just say I'm better at charming the ladies than I am at dealing with gentlemen."

Chapter Eight

At the Barkers' household the following morning, Mrs Barker was ecstatic to see a carriage pulling up outside.

"Oh my, girls, do come quickly! I do believe we are about to get some early morning visitors. If I'm not mistaken, it appears to be two gentlemen, two well-dressed gentlemen, if I'm not wrong," said Mrs Barker excitedly.

Kathleen hurried over to the window to get a good look.

"Oh my, Mary, you must come and take a look. I do believe it could well be Duke Cravendish and Lord Bloom."

"Mr Barker! Oh, where is your father when we have need of him?" said Mrs Barker.

"Good heavens, what is all this excitement about so early in the morning, ladies?" asked Mr Barker.

"Mr Barker, there you are! We do believe that Duke Cravendish and Lord Bloom are heading this way."

"Well, in that case, I will be in my study should you require me for anything," said Mr Barker.

Mrs Potters, the housekeeper, let them in.

"Mrs Barker, Duke Cravendish and Lord Bloom for you."

"Gentlemen, what an honour it is to welcome you into our home. Won't you please come in? I am sorry, we were not expecting you. Mr Barker is busy in his study at the moment; I will just go and check up on him, see if he's free. While I do that, would you gentlemen care for a tour of the estate? I'm sure Mary and Kathleen would be delighted to show you around."

"Won't you follow me, gentlemen?" said Kathleen eagerly.

Lord Bloom was eager to walk alongside Kathleen, leaving Mary to walk along with Duke Cravendish.

Kathleen was in her element conversing with Lord Bloom as they walked through the orchard together. Mary decided to drop back and give her sister space to talk to Lord Bloom without interference. Knowing that Kathleen was happily ahead and out of earshot, Mary felt free to ask Duke Cravendish a question.

"Duke Cravendish, may I ask you something? It's about Lord Bloom."

"Go ahead, ask me whatever you like about him."

"Well, it's in regard to Kathleen. Can she trust Lord Bloom? The thing is, Duke Cravendish, Kathleen is easily trusting and she sees the best in everybody, and I would hate for her to get hurt in any way."

"Miss Mary, I can assure you that Lord Bloom is not a rake or a scoundrel; he's a saint compared with other gentlemen I know. I can assure you that Lord Bloom's affections for your sister are real. The man is half besotted with her already. Now, Miss Mary, I suggest we continue walking before our presence is missed."

They had walked through the orchid and seen the lake,

stables and outbuilding and they were now returning back to the house half an hour later.

"Well, gentlemen, that is the tour of our humble estate. I am sure Papa will be free to see you both now," said Kathleen.

"Thank you. It was good to see what the area has to offer and what can be applied to the Cravendish estate's grounds," replied Lord Bloom.

Back at the front of the house, a new coach was parked up and was preparing to depart.

"Good heavens, more visitors!" said Kathleen.

They walked back into the front parlour room to see Mr Barker was now present and talking to another gentleman who was in the room.

"William!" cried Mary when she saw the other gentleman.

"Mary, there you are! I was expecting you to be here when I got back but Mrs Potters told me you were giving a tour," said William.

"Oh, William, if I had known you would be arriving today, I would have been waiting for you! So the carriage out front is yours?" asked Mary.

"It's not mine; however, I was dropped off in it. It must have just been leaving when you returned."

"William, my boy, let me introduce you to the newly titled Duke Cravendish and his companion Lord Bloom. This is my eldest son, William. Now, I believe you gentlemen are here to have a meeting with me, are you not? Come this way, gentlemen, my study's through here, and you better come along too, William, get your head in the business world," said Mr Barker.

"Quite a family you have for yourself, Mr Barker," said Duke Cravendish.

"Well, you've only met half of them. I've three other daughters already married and I've a younger son as well, Edward; he's away at school. However, I do believe you came to see me to talk about something other than my family. So how can I be of help to you two gentlemen?" asked Mr Barker.

"I've been informed, Mr Barker, that you know the Cravendish estate land better than anyone else in Cattleton. Mr Barker, I've seen what you've done with your own estate and I was hoping to restore the Cravendish estate to its former glory," stated Duke Cravendish.

"My, that will be a lot of work. It's not had much going on on it for a quite a while, I believe," said Mr Barker.

"I am aware of that, Mr Barker. That's why I've brought Lord Bloom up here to Cattleton with me to help manage the project."

"May I ask you, Duke Cravendish, what you need my father for and what he will get out of helping you?" asked William.

"Mr Barker, you know the land, while myself and Lord Bloom have no knowledge of the countryside. So, we require your expertise in such matters, in what will work and what will not work. I know my uncle wasn't in his right mind so he wouldn't have come to you for advice. You will have my gratitude and whatever else you require of me, Mr Barker."

"Well, Duke Cravendish, can I ask you something? Are you planning on spending much time here in the countryside?"

"Well, I plan on calling the Cravendish estate home, so I guess you can say the countryside is my new home now."

"How about you, Lord Bloom?"

"Well, I'm quite enjoying my time here in the countryside and am in no rush to leave."

"Splendid, I'm pleased to hear that gentlemen. Come and call on me any time you need me."

"Thank you, Mr Barker, you are too kind. We hope to host an evening when everything's all ready."

"We'll look forward to it, gentlemen; well, especially Mrs Barker. I will send over some men to help you out tomorrow. I have a feeling you will have need of them. I might even come and check out the estate myself. I've always had a hankering to see all of the Cravendish estate."

"Well, thanks again, Mr Barker. Until tomorrow then."

"Father, why are you allowing two gentlemen who you hardly know, and who you know hardly anything about, to come to you for help?" enquired William.

"William, this is just the way things work in the country. A neighbour in need is a friend indeed. William, has being in the Navy taught you to turn your back on your neighbours?"

"No, Father, it's just taught me to be wary of who to trust. You are far too trusting for your own good. You know next to nothing about these gentlemen," replied William.

"Mrs Barker, my dear, won't you tell William all you know of Duke Cravendish and Lord Bloom? William's concerned about my well-being in dealing with the gentlemen."

"Of course. Well, we first met Duke Cravendish by accident – or that's how he met Mary. They bumped into each other when we were leaving the dressmaker's and the conversation between them started straight away."

"Mother, I'm sure William doesn't need to know every single word that's been said between us and Duke Cravendish."

"Mary and Duke Cravendish have spent a lot of time together. They have performed together and danced with each other. Also, he's a man of the sea like you, William, but not in the Navy. He's also Lady Beatrice's nephew on her brother's side of the family. Well, as for Lord Bloom, he's just the nicest gentleman you could ever meet. Lord Bloom couldn't keep his eyes off Kathleen, they shared at least three dances, and he wouldn't see a lady without a dance partner," said Mrs Barker.

"See, William, when you decide to settle down and get married, you will now know how to keep a wife happy."

"Duke Cravendish and Lord Bloom are planning on staying in the countryside for quite some time, so that will please you, my dear. Of course, I'm sure Duke Cravendish will hold a ball at the Cravendish estate sometime in the future," said Mr Barker to his wife.

"Mary, won't you play for all of us? I've missed your playing while I've been away at sea. You don't really get the chance to enjoy music while you're on board a ship. By the way, Mary, I want to hear all about the new Duke Cravendish from you," said William.

"Such as what, William?"

"Well, Mother mentioned that he was a man of the sea. What was his rank in his previous occupation on the ship?" asked William.

"He was a captain of his own ship, I believe; that's what Lady Beatrice might have said," replied Mary.

"You're not saying to me that the new Duke Cravendish is, or was, the notorious Captain Cravendish?" asked William with concern in his voice.

"I'm sure Cravendish is a common surname. And William, you can't go around saying such things about a duke without proof."

"So, Mary are you trying to tell me that Captain Cravendish and Duke Cravendish are the same person and that you are acquainted with this gentleman? I know of this gentleman's reputation. The man likes a challenge; maybe he's befriended you because you're his next challenge."

"Yes, that is what I'm telling you William and I know all about his reputation and I'm not foolish enough to fall for Duke Cravendish's charms, so you have nothing to concern yourself with. So how long are you going to be here in Cattleton? How long is your shore leave?" enquired Mary, eager to change the conversation.

"I'm just here for a couple of weeks while the ship is in for inspection and maintenance and then I'll be returning back to the ship," replied William.

"Well then you will be able to keep an eye out for Duke Cravendish while you are here and see for yourself that I am in no danger," replied Mary.

Meanwhile, returning from the Barker estate and arriving back at the Cravendish estate, Duke Cravendish and Lord Bloom returned to the study to formulate a plan to improve the Cravendish estate. However, Hugh was eager to discuss how his friend reacted to seeing William Barker.

"Well, that look on your face, Dylan, was something

I never thought I would see on *your* face: the look of jealousy," said Hugh who was trying to provoke Dylan.

"What look? Hugh, I have no idea what you are talking about," replied Dylan.

"No, I saw the look on your face when Mary rushed past us to embrace William."

"Well, that might be because I didn't know that William was her brother."

"Maybe you should listen more. So you've not heard of William Barker before, then? *I've* heard of William Barker. He's quite high up in the Royal Navy. I'm surprised you haven't heard of him on your voyages."

"Well, Hugh, that might be because I go out of my way to avoid naval vessels."

"The next few weeks will be interesting, then, if William Barker is going to be here."

Chapter Nine

"Good morning, gentlemen. Mr Barker is here with four other gentlemen," said the housekeeper, Mrs Rodgers.

"Thank you. We will be right there."

"Mr Barker, good morning," said Duke Cravendish as he exited the house and greeted Mr Barker.

"Good morning, gentlemen. I brought three of my best men, and I also brought William along to give him some guidelines on estate management for future knowledge. Oh, I see the estate is in more disrepair than I first thought. Well, first thing you're going to need to do, Duke Cravendish, is hire more staff. I can ask around town, get you some more field hands, and you could do with getting some more household staff as well. I'm sure your aunt and Mrs Barker will help you out with hiring household staff. So, do you have many tenants here at the moment who you could put to work getting the estate restored? Because I'm sure in a few weeks' time we can get the grounds sorted out," said Mr Barker.

"Inside seems alright; most of the rooms have been

opened up and are now in use. Some rooms could still do with some sorting out. But apart from that, the inside of the house is in good condition."

"So you could hold a ball soon here at the Cravendish estate?" asked Mr Barker.

"Oh, I don't know about that, Mr Barker," replied Duke Cravendish.

"Nonsense. Mrs Barker won't let me leave here without securing a yes from you to holding a ball. It's the least you can do to return the favour, so to speak."

"You drive a hard bargain, Mr Barker."

"Dylan, I've sent out replies on your behalf to all your correspondence. We are expected to be in attendance at tonight's ball."

"So many balls. Must we attend all the balls that the village of Cattleton throws?"

"It's your duty as Duke Cravendish to attend such events."

"Can we not make our excuses and say we have a prior engagement?"

"Oh, that would be a shame."

"Why would that be a shame, Hugh?"

"Well, I have it on good authority that the Barker family will be there in attendance," said Hugh, who was eager to see Kathleen again.

"Is that you telling me to attend because you want to have the pleasure of seeing Miss Kathleen Barker again?" asked Dylan.

"Yes, I look forward to seeing her there. I feel she brightens my life and I could do with the support from you, my oldest friend," said Hugh.

"Alright, Hugh, we will go to the ball, put in an appearance and all that," replied Dylan.

"I'm sure your aunt will like it too," said Hugh.

"William, you don't have to keep an eye on me. And besides, William, it doesn't look like Duke Cravendish is here tonight. So why don't you go off and enjoy yourself, enjoy a game of cards? I know you are longing to play a hand or two whilst you are here," said Mary.

"You finally got William to leave your side then," said Kathleen as she came across to join Mary.

"Oh, Kathleen, I had to convince William that Duke Cravendish isn't here and will be unlikely to turn up to get him to leave my side. Has he now sent you over to keep an eye on me?" asked Mary.

"No, I was just coming over to check on you. Are you alright? Would you like to dance?"

"No, I am good thanks, Kathleen. I think I will go outside and get some air. The conversation in here is not improving my mood either. All people seem to be talking about is Duke Cravendish. I can't go anywhere without hearing his name," said Mary, feeling very irritated.

The cool night air gave a welcome release after being in the crowded ballroom. A few people were outside, but they were mainly courting couples wanting to get free time on their own. Mary moved on down the path, not wanting to end up an interloper.

"Sorry, I didn't see you there," said Mary as she nearly walked into somebody.

"Well, who do we have here?" asked Duke Cravendish.

"Duke Cravendish, I didn't know you were here this evening. Everybody has been wondering where you are."

"We've not long been here. Did you not see Lord Bloom inside?" enquired Duke Cravendish.

"No, I must have missed him," replied Mary.

"So, you didn't come looking for me then?" asked Duke Cravendish.

"No, I did nothing of the sort. It was warm in the ballroom so I stepped outside for some air and decided to get some privacy."

The sound of approaching voices was coming in their direction and, not wanting to be seen with Duke Cravendish by anybody, Mary did the first thing she could think of and pulled Duke Cravendish into the hedge maze.

"Oh my, Mary, I never took you for a coquette. Clearly what I've heard about you is not true," said Duke Cravendish, surprised by Mary's sudden movement.

"How dare you suggest such a thing about me? The only reason I dragged you into this hedge maze was because I didn't want to be seen with you," said Mary angrily.

Mary raised her hand, ready to slap him. She didn't care that Duke Cravendish was a duke; he had insulted her. But Duke Cravendish had quicker reflexes than Mary, and he caught her hand before she could strike her blow.

"I wouldn't do that if I was you," said Duke Cravendish.

"Well, I'm not you, am I?" replied Mary.

"Such buried passion you have, Mary, festering underneath the surface, just waiting to be unleashed."

Then Duke Cravendish was kissing the inside of Mary's wrist. His lips brushed gently over it. A shiver of desire passed through Mary. What was happening to her and why was she letting Duke Cravendish get so close? She then came to her senses and pushed Duke Cravendish back whilst telling him to stay away from her.

Mary rushed back inside before anybody could recall seeing her outside, hoping no one would notice that there was anything wrong. Mary scanned the room, on the lookout for Kathleen or Lord Bloom. Mary spotted them together at the refreshment table. Mary tried to compose herself quickly in the hope that Kathleen would not suspect anything to be wrong.

The feelings that Duke Cravendish had brought upon her were so unexpected and different.

"Oh my, Lord Bloom, it's good to see you again," said Mary as she approached Lord Bloom and Kathleen.

"Hello, Miss Mary. It's good to see you again too. May I serve you a glass of punch? I was just serving Miss Kathleen here some," asked Lord Bloom.

"No thank you, Lord Bloom. May I have a quiet word with you?" asked Mary.

"Of course, Miss Mary, is everything alright?" asked Lord Bloom with concern in his voice.

"Yes, I am quite alright. I wanted to have a word with you about Duke Cravendish."

"I see."

"Well, I saw him just a moment ago outside. I fear he may have had too much to drink. I left him in the garden by the entrance to the hedge maze."

"Right, well, thank you for sharing that information with me, Miss Mary. If you will forgive me, Miss Kathleen, I need to attend to some urgent business that has just cropped up. I hope not to be gone for too long."

"Mary, are you alright? You look flushed, like something's happened," enquired Kathleen.

"No, I am perfectly fine, Kathleen. Please don't ask me any questions and I'll tell you no lies. Also, Kathleen, please do not mention any of this to William, or speak to William about anything you might have heard about tonight's events. It will be a lot better for all concerned."

"If that's what you want me to do, Mary, I will, but what if William suspects something is wrong?"

"Well, if William does suspect anything then we will have to reassure him that everything's fine. Come, Kathleen, let's go and find the rest of our family so we can leave this ball. I'm sure we've been here long enough for it to be socially accepted."

"Shouldn't we wait for Lord Bloom to return? I would hate to miss saying goodnight to him."

"Oh, Kathleen, we don't know how long Lord Bloom's going to be. I have a feeling he is going to be gone a while. Look, I think I've spotted Father and William coming out of the card room."

"Mary, Kathleen, are you two having an enjoyable evening?" asked Mr Barker.

"Yes, it's been a wonderful night and we are now ready to leave. I presume you and William enjoyed your game of cards and were lucky enough to win on a good couple of hands?" said Mary.

"Yes, we've had a splendid evening as well. Now the hard part – getting your mother to leave," said Mr Barker.

"What the hell were you thinking of, Cravendish? I warned you about getting too close to Miss Mary. Luckily for you, she thought that you were intoxicated, but I can clearly see that you are not. So, did you at least think before you acted on your impulses?" asked Hugh.

"What is it that I'm supposed to have done?" asked Dylan.

"I think you know exactly what you did and for your sake, I hope her brother William doesn't find out what you did to his sister or he will be calling you out. It will be pistols at dawn."

"Mary is quite a delightful character to know," said Dylan.

"Is that all you have to say for yourself on the subject? You do know you could have compromised her?" said Hugh, concerned for Mary.

"I can assure you, I didn't come close to compromising her. Clearly I had more of an effect on Mary than I originally thought. That's a very interesting thing to know."

"I know that look you have, Cravendish, and I know you're plotting something in that head of yours. I will not be party to whatever you have planned."

"Now, Hugh, shall we go inside so people see that I'm here attending this ball and not just hiding out here in the garden?"

"Duke Cravendish, we're so pleased you could make it; we were concerned you wouldn't be able to attend," said Mrs Sedgewick who was tonight's host.

"Sorry for my lateness. A prior engagement took me longer than expected, then I was admiring your grounds. But I'm here now. I hope I've not missed too much of this evening's entertainment?"

"Not at all, Duke Cravendish. Now that you're here I'm sure the evening can get fully underway. Your aunt has been singing your praises all week, Duke Cravendish."

"Yes, my aunt does seem to be singing my praises all over town."

Chapter Ten

Later that night, Mary slept fitfully. Her dreams were full of Duke Cravendish. Mary's first dream was of herself back in the hedge maze with Duke Cravendish. However, in the dream Duke Cravendish was kissing more than just the inside of her wrist; he was kissing her fully on the mouth. The version of herself in her dreams was behaving nothing like Mary's normal self; in fact, the Mary in her dream was behaving more like Linda, her youngest sister. She was half expecting to morph into Linda, and then in her vision she was kissing Duke Cravendish, though she remained Mary, and she wasn't pushing Duke Cravendish away, she was just letting him devour her. Then the Duke in Mary's dream spoke to her in a sweet, seductive way. *May we be good lovers together, Mary.* He gave her a passionate kiss.

With that, Mary awoke feeling as though she was burning up as if she had been in the fires of hell.

"Morning, Mary. You look dreadful," said Kathleen.

"Thanks for that, Kathleen."

"No, I mean, are you alright? You're not sick, are you? I woke up in the night to hear you mumbling in your sleep."

"What was it I was saying?" asked Mary.

"I don't know, Mary, your words were mumbled."

"Do I have a fever at all, Kathleen? I feel as though I'm burning up."

"No, you don't feel hot, Mary. Maybe it was just bad dreams that made you feel unwell."

"Good morning, my girls. Is it not a lovely morning? Oh Mary, my dear, you look dreadful. I hope you're not coming down with anything," said Mrs Barker as the girls took their seats at the table.

"No, I am quite alright, Mother. I just slept fitfully; bad dreams, that's all," replied Mary.

"Well, that's good to hear. We wouldn't want to have you laid up with something when my baby Linda is travelling up from Brighton to pay us a visit. If only your father would let me visit Brighton, then Linda wouldn't have to travel up here to be with us. I told her she shouldn't be travelling so far in her condition, but Linda assures me she wouldn't have it any other way."

"How wonderful for you, Mother, to have half your children under the same roof just for a little while," said William.

"Oh, William, you're quite right, it will be just wonderful."

"Right, well, if that is all, I will just go for a morning walk, clear away the cobwebs from my mind," said Mary.

"Well, Mary, just be careful. It looks like a storm is approaching," said William with concern in his voice.

"Oh, William, you do worry too much. But I promise not to go too far away."

"Are you sure you wouldn't like some company on your walk?" asked William.

"No, I would rather be on my own. I'm not the best of company at the moment, I want to clear my mind. Thank you for the offer though, William. I'm sure it's still safe enough for me to walk alone in the countryside, is it not?"

"No, you are quite right, Mary. The countryside is still safe to walk in alone."

Mary had been so busy processing her thoughts that she had lost track of where she was. She remembered walking the outskirts of her father's property line but now she was in a wooded area that didn't look familiar to her. Then she ended up tripping on a fallen tree branch. Mary felt a pain rush through her ankle and tried to stand up but the pain in her ankle was too great.

Mary shouted out for help, hoping there would be someone in the area to hear her cries for help.

"Hello, is anyone here?" Duke Cravendish called out. He was sure he had heard a woman's voice.

Mary heard a voice in the distance.

"Over here! If you could help me up," Mary shouted out.

"Well, if it isn't Mary," said Duke Cravendish as he approached Mary and assessed the situation.

"Duke Cravendish. Great, it's you!" said Mary, annoyed that her rescuer was the last person she wanted to see.

"That's not a very friendly greeting for someone who's coming to your rescue," said Duke Cravendish.

"I'm sorry, please forgive my rudeness. If you could just see it in yourself to help me up, thank you, Duke Cravendish," said Mary.

"I would stay off that ankle for a while, just in case

you've done more than just sprained it," advised Duke Cravendish.

"I will. I intend to limp back the way I came," replied Mary.

"You do know a storm is coming? Have you looked up at the sky recently?"

And sure enough, the bright blue sky that had been out earlier to tempt Mary out on her walk, had now changed to a darker shade of blue.

"Allow me to help you, Mary?" asked Duke Cravendish.

"No, I'm fine on my own, Duke Cravendish," replied Mary.

"You do make things difficult for yourself, don't you?" said Duke Cravendish.

"Duke Cravendish, what are you doing? Put me down right now!" exclaimed Mary as Duke Cravendish scooped her off her feet in the same way a newly married man would lift his new bride up and carry her over the threshold.

"A storm is coming, Mary. I'm getting us to shelter as quickly as possible so we don't end up drowning in the storm. There's a little shack up ahead. I spotted it when I was taking in the whole of the estate with your father," said Duke Cravendish.

"So, this is all part of your property?" enquired Mary.

"Yes, it is. Well, here we are. We can shelter here until the storm passes."

"You can put me down now then," said Mary.

"You know, we wouldn't have made it here in time if I hadn't carried you. Now, would you allow me to examine your ankle and check for any damage?" asked Duke Cravendish.

"I don't think you should do that. Do you know what you're doing?" asked Mary.

"Trust me, Mary, I've seen my fair share of injuries in my time."

Before Mary could say another word, Duke Cravendish had taken her ankle in his hands.

"Tell me if this hurts at all. Well, the good news is that you've not broken anything; it's just badly sprained. You won't be able to walk on it for a while though."

"It's just what I thought. I will just limp back home after this storm passes."

"Do you hate being in my company that much that you would risk injuring yourself further to get away from me? No, Mary, I will help you up to the main house and then I will get Lord Bloom to see you safely home in the carriage."

"Well then, I thank you for your plan and I greatly appreciate it."

"While we're stuck in here together, maybe we should talk to pass the time. So, I believe you and my aunt are close acquaintances. She speaks very highly of you."

"Well, it first started in the music shop where I was introduced to Lady Beatrice. We got talking and discovered we had quite a lot in common, and since then I have been visiting Lady Beatrice at least once a week. She enjoys listening to me play and she misses being able to play herself. I never knew Lady Beatrice's family's surname until she introduced me to you. She mentioned having family down in Bristol and she was interested in what her family were up to. I think Lady Beatrice believes you were a merchant ship man rather than someone who ran his own ship."

"Well, it is more or less what I did until my inheritance

came in. I never really knew my uncle. My father never mentioned him. I believe they had a fallout many years ago and clearly my uncle was of sound enough mind when writing his will to cut my father out."

"So, I take it your father was angry when you inherited the title and not him?" asked Mary.

"I wouldn't know. I've not spoken to my father for many years. We're not a close family, not like your family. I suppose that's why I am so protective of my friendship with Hugh. We first met at school and we've been close friends ever since. Hugh's family has been like a family to me. His father passed away a couple of years ago and he's had to deal with such a lot. So, when I found out I was to come up here, I invited Hugh up to give him time away."

"Lord Bloom's friendship means a great deal to you."

"Does it surprise you that I have feelings and I care about other people? I do believe the rain has about stopped. Maybe we should make our way up to the main house. Are you ready to lean on me to take the weight off your ankle?"

"Is it far to the main house?"

"It's quite a way for you to limp."

They arrived at the main house in just a short time, where a servant greeted them.

"Duke Cravendish, sir, are you alright?"

"Hello. Yes, I'm well. However, would you be kind enough to track down Lord Bloom and let him know his presence is needed in the drawing room? And would you kindly ask Annie to bring in some tea?" instructed Duke Cravendish.

"Yes, Duke Cravendish, sir, I'll get on to that straight away," replied the servant.

"Mary, won't you sit down and rest your foot on this stool? Keep the weight off your ankle," instructed Duke Cravendish.

"Dylan, what the hell happened to you? I've been waiting for you in the study for ages," said Lord Bloom as he entered the room.

"Sorry, Hugh, I got caught out in the storm and as you can see, we are not alone."

"Miss Mary, I'm sorry, I didn't see you there. Have you been here long?" enquired Lord Bloom.

"I'm sorry, Lord Bloom, it's my fault that Duke Cravendish wasn't where he was meant to be. He happened to come across me in the woods. I had foolishly tripped over and sprained my ankle on a fallen branch. I was calling out for help when Duke Cravendish found me and came to my aid," explained Mary.

"Do you need us to send for the doctor?" asked Lord Bloom.

"No, everything's fine. It's just a sprain," replied Mary.

Mary left out the part about Duke Cravendish having examined her ankle already. Then, a moment later, a servant came in with some tea.

"Miss Mary, how do you take your tea?" asked Lord Bloom.

"Milk and just a little sugar, please," replied Mary.

"So, what happened to your chaperone, Miss Mary?" asked Lord Bloom.

"Oh, I don't go out with a chaperone. Things are more relaxed here in the countryside; it's not like being in a city where a young lady requires a chaperone."

"But surely a lady on her own needs to be careful. One never knows who they are likely to run into."

"Lord Bloom, you really worry too much, you're just like William. Though I can understand as you have a younger sister yourself. Duke Cravendish told me so earlier."

"That's true, I'm an older brother and I guess I can't help but worry about young ladies."

"The countryside is perfectly safe for one to walk alone in the daytime. Well, I have imposed upon your kind hospitality for far too long, and I see the sunshine has now reappeared."

"Lord Bloom, I said you would be more than accommodating to see Miss Mary home safely in the carriage. I've advised Miss Mary not to put weight upon her ankle."

"Of course, it would be my honour to do so, Miss Mary."

Chapter Eleven

The carriage rolled up outside of the Barkers' residence, where Kathleen, on hearing the sound of horses, came running out of the house.

"It's Mary!" she cried out and William came running out after her.

"Oh, Mary, whatever has happened to you? You've been gone all morning. We were beginning to get worried about you," said Kathleen.

Then Kathleen spotted Duke Cravendish and Lord Bloom and blushed scarlet at the sight of the two gentlemen.

"Gentlemen, it's good to see you both again. What brings you here today?" asked Kathleen.

"Well, we came across Miss Mary here in the rain and she had sprained her ankle in a fall. We couldn't let her limp home, so we decided to give her a lift back here," replied Duke Cravendish.

"Mary, here, let me help you down. You can lean on me," said William as he looked up at Duke Cravendish with a scowl on his face.

"Thank you, William. Thank you again for your help, Duke Cravendish and Lord Bloom," said Mary.

"Would you gentlemen like to stay for tea? I'm sure Mama wouldn't mind if you wanted to partake in a cup of tea," asked Kathleen.

"Thank you for the kind offer, Miss Kathleen, but myself and Lord Bloom really must be going. We only dropped by to see Miss Mary safely home," replied Duke Cravendish.

"Well, thank you once again, gentlemen, for seeing my sister home safely," said William.

"You weren't expecting it to be me, were you, Kathleen? You thought it was Linda arriving."

"Yes, Mama told me to be on the lookout for Linda's imminent arrival."

"Is that my Linda I hear arriving?" said Mrs Barker in an excited voice.

"No Mother, it's just me, Mary."

"She was just with Duke Cravendish and Lord Bloom. They rescued Mary when she got caught in the rain," said Kathleen.

"It's lucky they came across you. You clearly planned your walk well," said Mrs Barker.

"I didn't plan on having to have anyone help me," said Mary.

"Did you not invite them in?" asked Mrs Barker.

"Kathleen did but they needed to get going."

"Never mind. My Linda will be here soon enough."

The sounds of another carriage arriving filled the air.

"She's finally here, my baby, Linda," said Mrs Barker excitedly.

"Mama, who was that I happened to pass on my way here in the poshest carriage I've seen for a while?" said Linda as she entered the house.

"Oh, Linda, it must have been Duke Cravendish and Lord Bloom," said Mrs Barker.

"So that was the new Duke Cravendish. I heard talk about him during my journey here. Handsome gentleman, I must say, and single by all accounts," said Linda.

"Of course, you will have a chance to meet him at tonight's ball," said Mrs Barker.

"I'm sure Linda won't want to attend a ball, not after such a long journey and certainly not in her condition," said Mary.

"Oh, Mary, I'll be fine for this evening. I will have a good rest this afternoon and will be fully functional to attend tonight's ball," replied Linda.

"The mail cart is here. Oh my, I see we've got another wedding invitation! It's from Mrs Tempest; her daughter Caitlin is to marry the Miners' son. I'm sure Mrs Tempest will be lording it over me this evening; another daughter of hers getting married while two of my daughters are still unwed," said Mrs Barker.

"You know the old saying, Mama, *going to one wedding brings on another*. So, we can only hope that Kathleen will be the next to marry, should Lord Bloom or Duke Cravendish make her an offer sometime soon," said Linda.

"Let's hope you're right, Linda. Let's hope the wedding season is upon us."

"Well, it wouldn't be much of a wedding season without a good few weddings," joked William as he entered the room.

"Oh my!" cried Mary as she was reading a letter that she had received.

"Mary, what is wrong?" asked Mrs Barker.

"Nothing's wrong! It's a letter from my friend Marinea; she wishes for me to visit her in Bath. She longs for me to meet her husband and wishes for me to come down at my earliest convenience."

"How do you expect to travel down to Bath, Mary, when you are quite clearly needed here?" asked Mrs Barker.

"Mother, you have no need of me here, you just don't want me to go," said Mary.

"What's all this commotion going on in here?" said Mr Barker as he entered the room.

"Mary's got it into her head that she can just run off to Bath to spend time with Marinea," said Mrs Barker.

"I don't see the harm in Mary going to Bath. William's still here for another week; they can travel down to Salisbury together and then they can part ways with not too far left to travel on to Bath," said Mr Barker.

"Thank you, Father, I believe I have your permission to go. In that case, I'll go write a reply to Marinea now," said Mary excitedly.

"Mr Barker, how could you agree to such a thing? You know Mary needs to be here," said Mrs Barker, now annoyed with Mr Barker.

"Mary is a grown woman who makes up her own mind. At least this way, William, you will be with her to keep her safe on the journey."

"Yes, but Duke Cravendish is here," replied Mrs Barker.

"And he will probably still be here when Mary returns from Bath. Maybe being in Marinea's company will change Mary's mind where marriage is concerned," said Mr Barker.

"Oh well, I just hope you're right, Mr Barker. I would hate for my well-laid plans to go to waste."

The evening of another ball was here and Mary was talking to Lady Beatrice.

"Mary, hello. I hear you are soon to be leaving us to visit Bath?" asked Lady Beatrice.

"Yes, that's true, Lady Beatrice, though Mother doesn't approve of me going," replied Mary.

"I'm sure your mother will come round to the idea soon enough," said Lady Beatrice as if she knew something that Mary didn't know.

Meanwhile, across other side of the room, Linda and her mother are discussing the current ballroom.

"Oh my, what a splendid room they have here! So much has changed since I was last here at a ball. Do let me know, Mama, when you spot Duke Cravendish and Lord Bloom. I would quite like an introduction," said Linda.

"I do believe you are about to get your wish, Linda. I think I see them just arriving now. I will get them to come over and meet you," said Mrs Barker.

"Mrs Barker, it's good to see you again."

"Let me introduce you to my youngest daughter, Linda."

"It's an honour to meet you," said Lord Bloom.

"Duke Cravendish, may I have a word with you in private?" said William.

"Oh, William, how rude of you to steal Duke Cravendish away when we have only just met!" exclaimed Linda.

"How can I help you, William?" asked Duke Cravendish.

"It's about Mary. I wish to thank you for coming to her aid yesterday. However, I want you to keep your distance from her in the future. I don't know what game you're playing but my sister Mary is off limits to the likes of you," said William, making sure his feelings were known.

"William, I can assure you your sister's a grown woman and she can make up her own mind. Perhaps I should tell you I am due to leave town in a few days' time to go back to Bristol, so I'll be safely away from Mary. Lord Bloom is staying here to look after the Cravendish estate, but I'm sure you won't have a problem with his presence around your sister," replied Duke Cravendish.

"William, what's going on here?" asked Mary as she came across the pair of them.

"Nothing, Mary, Duke Cravendish and I were just talking about shipping," replied William.

"Well, in that case, I'm pleased I interrupted you. William, won't you partake of a dance with me?" said Mary as she steers William off in the direction of the dance floor.

"William, I'm not stupid. I know you and Duke Cravendish were not discussing ships; you were telling him to stay away from me. You don't trust me not to have good instincts of my own."

"Mary, you're my sister. I care about your well-being, that is all."

"Believe me, William, I know what sort of gentleman Duke Cravendish is and I have no intention of getting mixed up with him. How many times do I need to tell you so?"

A few days later at the Cravendish estate, Duke Cravendish was packing to leave Cattleton and return to Bristol when Hugh walked in.

"Dylan, you can't leave just yet; we're expected at a

wedding. And what's the rush? Was it something to do with what William Barker was wanting to talk to you about the other day?" asked Hugh in a concerned manner.

"No, I received a letter from Skip yesterday morning," replied Dylan.

"That's your second-in-command on your ship, if I remember correctly," said Hugh.

"I was stupid to leave him in charge. Something has gone wrong and I need to leave and sort everything out down in Bristol. I wanted to talk with you about leaving you here in charge of the Cravendish estate; make it your home, stay as long as you want."

"When will you be coming back?" asked Hugh.

"I don't know, Hugh, it will take as long as it takes. You know I'm not a fan of weddings or churches. For that matter, it will be better if I'm not here," said Dylan.

"People will take it as an insult if you don't attend; your Aunt Beatrice will be annoyed with me if you don't show," replied Hugh.

"You're afraid of my aunt, then? Alright, we will go to this wedding but by the end of the day, I will be heading back to Bristol," said Dylan, making it clear that he would definitely be leaving.

"What a wonderful service. I've always loved a good wedding. It's just a shame it wasn't one of my daughters getting married," said Mrs Barker.

"Now, Mama, I wish there were more single gentlemen in Cattleton for my dear sisters," said Linda.

"Mary, will you come with me? I do believe I've just seen a dear friend of ours," said Kathleen as she took Mary's arm and they crossed to the other side of the room.

"Oh, Mary, how could I have been so blind as not to notice that Linda is just like Mama?" said Kathleen.

"Oh, Kathleen, you can't blame yourself for not picking up on such things. Besides, you're still young."

"Lord Bloom, there you are. It's good to see you here. Did you enjoy the service?" asked Kathleen.

"Very much so. I'm a big fan of weddings; I love seeing people united together," replied Lord Bloom.

"So, do you see yourself staying in Cattleton for a long period of time or are you likely to be moving on soon now that the Cravendish estate is doing so well?" asked Kathleen.

"I have no intentions of leaving anytime soon, Miss Kathleen. I see you ladies don't have anything to drink. May I fetch you both a drink?" asked Lord Bloom.

"You are too kind, Lord Bloom," replied Kathleen.

"If you excuse me, ladies, I will be back soon with your drinks."

Lord Bloom approaches the drinks table to discover that Dylan is just standing there.

"Dylan, what are you doing here, hiding out at the drinks table?"

"I'm avoiding everybody and hoping to get out of here as soon as possible," replied Dylan.

"Here, you can help me give this drink to Miss Mary," said Lord Bloom as he led the way back to where the ladies were waiting.

"There you go, Miss Kathleen, Miss Mary."

"Duke Cravendish, it's good to see you. Did you enjoy the service?" asked Kathleen.

"I'm not a fan of weddings but Lord Bloom said I would disappoint my aunt if I didn't attend. Miss Mary, will you accompany me outside for some fresh air? I do believe it is mighty warm in here," said Duke Cravendish.

Mary looked around to make sure William wasn't watching her before agreeing to go outside with Duke Cravendish.

"I'm sorry to drag you away from your sister, but I do believe Lord Bloom is eager to spend time alone with Miss Kathleen. Just between us, I believe that Lord Bloom is quite smitten with your sister."

"I believe that's something we can agree on," replied Mary.

"I'm pleased I will be able to leave him in charge of the Cravendish estate."

"I never took you for one to have romantic match-making on your mind. Why would you need to leave Lord Bloom in charge of the Cravendish estate unless you were leaving? Are you planning on leaving Cattleton? Please tell me it isn't because of the conversation that you had with William last night, is it?" asked Mary.

"No, though I'm sure William would like it if it was. No, I'm leaving because I've got some business to take care of back in Bristol."

"So, we are not going to see each for quite some time then. I'm sure my mother will be disappointed that you're not going to be around. But I suppose it's good news for Kathleen that Lord Bloom will be staying in Cattleton. So, when are you planning on leaving?" asked Mary.

"Tomorrow morning," replied Duke Cravendish.

Chapter Twelve

A few days later at the Barker household, Mary and William were getting ready to depart for the carriage that would take them to Salisbury when Mrs Barker decided to speak to Mary properly for the first time since Mr Barker had agreed to let Mary go off to Bath.

"Well, I suppose it's all working out well. Duke Cravendish left for Bristol a few days ago, so I guess I don't have to worry about you going off to Bath now after all. Besides, your father tells me Bath isn't that far away from Bristol, so maybe there could be a chance of you meeting Duke Cravendish there. Of course, I didn't tell William that; for some reason I get the feeling that William doesn't like Duke Cravendish, but I don't know why," said Mrs Barker.

"Are you all ready for the off? I'm sure you will need to get going soon to catch the carriage?" said Mr Barker.

"Yes, well, we had better be going," said William.

"Take care. We look forward to hearing all about Bath," said Kathleen.

"And you, Kathleen. I hope everything goes well

between you and Lord Bloom whilst I'm away and I hope Linda's not too much of a handful," said Mary, whispering the end of the sentence.

"Miss Mary, I'm pleased I caught you before you left. May I help you on with your belongings?" asked Lord Bloom, who had just approached them.

"Oh, thank you, Lord Bloom. What are you doing here?" asked Mary.

"I was in town picking up supplies and heard you were off to Bath today, so I thought I would come across and wish you well on your journey, I hear the Cotswolds are really nice this time of year," said Lord Bloom.

"Well, thank you again, Lord Bloom," replied Mary.

"Mary, we better get on board before they leave without us," said William.

The carriage was fairly quiet with just one more traveller on board.

"Mary, you should get some rest while you can. It's going to be a long journey," said William.

"Oh, William, what utter nonsense! How can I think of resting when there is so much unexplored countryside to see on the journey?" replied Mary.

Meanwhile, down in Bath, Duke Cravendish had just arrived that very morning to have a respite at a regular stop-off point on his journey to Bristol. The tavern owner came running out when he spotted Captain Cravendish.

"Captain Cravendish, are you not a sight for sore eyes! A messenger dropped this off for you earlier. Looks like they were expecting your arrival," said the tavern owner.

Duke Cravendish recognised the writing as Skip's.

Everything has been dealt with now so there is no need to rush back. Great, Dylan thought. He had travelled back so quickly, and for what? Dylan left his belongings in his room and thought to explore Bath now that he had some time on his hands.

"Cravendish, is that you? It's me, Richard Miller," said Richard as he was walking towards Dylan.

"Yes it's me, Richard. How's everything with you? Married life treating you well?" asked Dylan.

"It couldn't be better. Marinea makes my life feel complete. You should try it yourself. So, Cravendish, what are you doing back here in Bath?" asked Richard. "I thought you had moved on to a new adventure with a title and all that."

"It's true, I've a title now. I'm now known as Duke Cravendish of Cattleton, a village in Derbyshire in the Midlands. I rushed back on some business matters that Skip brought up, and then he wrote to me here and told me it's all sorted, and there is now no need for me to rush back. Well, I will need to marry sometime if I want to keep the title, but I don't think I will get as lucky as you, Richard."

"Well, if you don't have to rush off to Bristol, why don't you come and stay with me and Marinea rather than in this place?"

"I'm sure your house is lovely but I wouldn't want to impose on you and your good wife."

"You wouldn't be imposing and Marinea's been looking forward to having people stay. A friend of Marinea's is arriving in a few days' time so it will be good to have another man at the dinner table. And besides, we have a lot of catching up to do. It's been far too long, has it not?"

It wasn't long before they arrived at the Miller residence which was among a crescent of other houses. They entered the house and Richard called out to his wife.

"Marinea, we've now got another member to add to our party. I would like to introduce you to an old school friend of mine. We've not seen each other for some time. Dylan Cravendish, my wife Marinea."

"Hello, it's nice to meet you, Dylan. Where is it you've come from?" asked Marinea.

"I've spent most of my life in Bristol, but I've recently inherited the title of Duke Cravendish and moved to a village in Derbyshire in the Midlands."

"So you're the new Duke Cravendish of Cattleton? Or is there another area in Derbyshire that has a Duke Cravendish?"

"No, you're correct. I am now Duke Cravendish of Cattleton. You are well informed about Cattleton."

"I see Richard didn't mention the small fact that Richard and I actually met in Cattleton and that my family are from Cattleton."

"No, he didn't mention that little fact. So, this friend you have coming to visit, is she from Cattleton as well?" asked Dylan.

"Yes, she is, perhaps the two of you have met already. Her name's Mary Barker."

"Yes, I'm acquainted with Miss Mary Barker."

"Oh, how marvellous. We won't have to introduce you to each other."

Chapter Thirteen

Three days later, the carriage arrived in Salisbury at a local inn run by a man and his wife. The innkeeper's wife had been informed to keep an eye out for Mary while she waited for the coach that would take her on to Bath.

"Hello, you must be Miss Mary. Please come with me, we have a ladies' waiting room set up in the back. I'll make sure she's protected, Mr Barker, until the carriage for Bath arrives," said the innkeeper's wife.

"Well, Mary, this is Salisbury. Here we part company. The innkeeper's wife here will keep an eye on you until your carriage comes. I have friends who visit Bath; I have already sent word to them to keep an eye out for you. I hope you have a nice time with Marinea in Bath and I'll see you next time I'm on leave," said William before he departed for his coach.

"Thank you, William. Take care of yourself," said Mary.

The coach was fuller than the carriage to Salisbury had been, though it wasn't too full. Mary had just got off the coach in Bath when she heard Marinea call out her name.

"Mary, I'm so pleased you could make it!" cried out Marinea as she spotted Mary in the crowd.

"Marinea! I hope you've not been waiting long?" asked Mary.

"It's been so long since I last saw you, Mary. I hope you don't mind but my husband has invited a friend to stay as well."

"Oh, of course not, Marinea; it's your house, not mine. Your husband is more than welcome to invite his friends to stay."

"I should warn you, Mary, so you don't get a shock… the friend in question is Duke Cravendish. He said that the two of you are acquainted already."

"Yes, that's correct, we are acquainted," replied Mary, who deliberately left her answer short.

Duke Cravendish was here in Bath. *Why isn't he in Bristol like he was supposed to be? And why is he always turning up in places where I am going to be?* thought Mary to herself.

"That's wonderful news, but don't keep me hanging. I want to hear all about how you and Duke Cravendish became acquainted. But tell me later, when we are in the privacy of the house."

It was just a short journey to the Millers' house.

"So, now that we are alone in private, tell me all about Duke Cravendish. I know he's handsome and so charming for a start. So, what I really want to know is, how did you end up becoming acquainted with him?" asked Marinea.

"Do you remember Lady Beatrice? Well, it turns out Duke Cravendish is her nephew. I was visiting Lady Beatrice when Duke Cravendish turned up, and then the next time we literally bumped into each other in town, and then Mother met Duke Cravendish, and you can guess my mother's interest. Duke Cravendish also came to my rescue when I was injured in the woods, and that's how we became acquainted really," said Mary.

"Well, I think there is more to this story than you're letting on but I will accept your story for now. Though, Mary, I look forward to seeing the two of you together later. The gentlemen should be back shortly. We have arranged a trip to the opera this evening; something new for you to experience. It's a must-see. I told Richard all about your love of music and I know you're going to enjoy it," said Marinea.

"Have you been to many operas then, Marinea?" asked Mary.

"We've been lucky enough to see a couple of performances. It is a very popular pastime. Many people flock to Bath for the waters and for the performances, you know," said Marinea.

"Well, do you think I have anything suitable to wear to such an event?" asked Mary.

"I'm sure we can find something suitable for you to wear. I'll bet your mother has put a fresh new gown in your luggage."

"What makes you think that, Marinea?"

"I know your mother, Mary. Trust me, she will have gone through your luggage. And so she has, judging by this gown, unless your tastes have changed over the last year? I'll send in my maid to help you get ready."

"Really, Marinea, there is no need. I can manage on my own."

"So you are still the same. You've not changed one bit, Mary."

"What do you mean by that, Marinea?"

"I just mean you're so independent and you don't want anyone to help you."

"Mary it's good to finally meet you. Marinea has talked about you quite a lot; I feel as though we've met already," said Mr Miller.

"It's good to meet you, Mr Miller," said Mary.

"Please call me Richard."

"Richard, that's something Miss Mary can't do. She likes to stay formal at all times," said Duke Cravendish.

"Well, maybe one day that will change and you'll be happy to call me Richard."

"Duke Cravendish, it's nice to see you again, though I thought you were going to Bristol?" asked Mary.

"My plans were changed, Miss Mary."

"With it being Mary's first time visiting the Opera it will be a good idea to arrive early," said Marinea.

"Then we better get going," said Mr Miller.

"Well, Miss Mary, you're in for a real treat," said Duke Cravendish.

Chapter Fourteen

"Come, Mary, we are up here. Richard's family owns their own box," said Marinea.

"Oh my, we are so high up yet we still get to see everything. It's certainly a breathtaking sight to see; I never imagined it would be like this," said Mary, impressed by her surroundings.

"It certainly is impressive, especially for a first visit, Mary, and I do believe they have themselves a full house tonight," said Marinea.

"We better take our seats as the performance will be starting soon," said Mr Miller.

"Ladies and gentlemen of Bath, welcome to tonight's opening performance of *The Magic Flute*."

"So, Miss Mary, how did you enjoy your first opera experience?" asked Duke Cravendish as they got up to leave the box and return to the main foyer.

"I believe I am a lover of opera already! I mean, the music just flows through me; it feels as though it's communicating with me. The music and singing combine into this magical performance. You can see the interaction between the two of them. Have they performed together for a while?" asked Mary.

"Yes, Madam Boulagise and Anton have performed together over the years and toured and travelled all over the world, but this is the first time they have performed this opera," replied Duke Cravendish.

"I would never have guessed you know so much about opera, Duke Cravendish," said Mary.

"Well, Miss Mary, if you would only allow yourself to get to know me you would learn a great deal more about me," replied Duke Cravendish.

They were then interrupted by a gentleman who had also been attending the opera and then he spoke to them.

"I'm sorry, I couldn't help overhearing your conversation. Are you Miss Mary Barker, by any chance?" enquired Mr Hartwell.

"Yes, that's me. Do we know each other, sir?" asked Mary.

"I'm sorry, do forgive me, I've not introduced myself. My name is John Hartwell. I'm a fellow Navy man like your brother, William. He sent word to me that his sister Mary would be visiting Bath and that you have a love of music. I was hoping you would be here tonight. I wasn't certain it was you until I heard your companion mention your name," said Mr Hartwell.

"Please forgive me, Mr Hartwell. Let me introduce you to Mr and Mrs Miller. I'm staying with them while I'm visiting Bath. And this is Mr Dylan."

"It's nice to meet you all. Now that we've met formally, I was wondering if it would be alright with Mr and Mrs Miller here if I were to call upon you during your stay here in Bath? I look forward to meeting you again soon, Miss

Mary. Thank you for your time, Mr and Mrs Miller, Mr Dylan," said Mr Hartwell, who then bid them farewell.

"Mr Dylan? Really, Mary, you didn't want to introduce me by my proper name?"

"You know perfectly well how William reacted when he heard your name mentioned. I would expect Mr Hartwell to react in the same way as William. And besides, I wouldn't want Mr Hartwell to write to William telling him that you are here in Bath as well because, knowing William, he will have me sent home as soon as possible."

"If you'll excuse me, Richard, ladies, I'll be back in a moment," said Duke Cravendish as he spotted Madam Boulagise watching them.

"So, what's William's problem with Duke Cravendish?" asked Marinea once Duke Cravendish was out of earshot.

"It's all to do with his past in shipping, and William also has ideas in his head that Duke Cravendish will try and seduce me because he likes a challenge, which is ridiculous as I have no interest in such matters," said Mary.

"Are you sure you have no interest in Duke Cravendish, Mary?" questioned Marinea.

"Of course. I'm sure we couldn't be any more opposite," replied Mary.

"They do say opposites attract. Not to mention how charming he is," said Marinea.

"Charming he may be, but he still won't be charming me," replied Mary.

"Cravendish, it's good see you again, though I wasn't expecting to see you here – at least, for a long time. Skip said you had moved to the Midlands, of all places," said Madam Boulagise.

"Well, I wouldn't be here now if it wasn't for Skip, if he spent less time talking and more time doing what he should be doing," said Dylan.

"So, you are here on *Captain* Cravendish business and not *Duke* Cravendish business. Are you pursuing the young miss that you are with this evening? I was going to say she's not your usual type; too pure, for one thing," said Madam Boulagise.

"It was good to see you again, Madam Boulagise. If you'll excuse me, I need to return to my party," said Dylan as he left Madam Boulagise.

"Cravendish, my door is always open if you would like to call on me," said Madam Boulagise.

"Duke Cravendish, was that Madam Boulagise who you were just conversing with, the singer of tonight's performance?" asked Mary.

"It was. She is an old acquaintance of mine," replied Duke Cravendish.

"And you didn't think of introducing us to her?" said Mary.

"Trust me, Miss Mary, Madam Boulagise isn't the type of female you should be conversing with."

"Why ever not? Just because she is a female with free will who makes her living by singing? Really, Duke Cravendish, you are as bad as William, judging a person by their profession."

"And I think we should have this conversation somewhere more private. Shall we go before we get trapped here? The carriage will be waiting out front," said Duke Cravendish.

A lot of carriages were already queuing up to leave the theatre district of Bath.

"Miss Mary, Marinea, allow me to help you in," said Duke Cravendish.

"Thank you, Duke Cravendish. My, it is busy! Clearly we are later leaving than I thought," said Marinea.

"It was certainly a fully packed out theatre tonight," said Mr Miller.

"You are free to move on now," said a guard who was organising all the carriages to make sure no one collided.

Chapter Fifteen

The carriage pulled up outside the Millers' front door. Marinea was quick to pick up on the tension between her friend Mary and Duke Cravendish.

"Richard, I feel as though we should retire for the night."

Mr and Mrs Miller exchanged knowing looks with each other.

"Right you are, Marinea."

And the couple headed upstairs after bidding goodnight to their guests. Duke Cravendish waited until the footfalls of Mr and Mrs Miller had faded away before he rounded on Mary.

"I've never known a female who is as naive as you. The reason I wouldn't introduce you to Madam Boulagise is because she isn't a woman like you; she's a woman of loose morals and she certainly isn't pure," said Duke Cravendish.

"I see. I suppose it isn't a good idea to introduce another female to one of your conquests, is it?"

"Oh, and that isn't the only thing you are naive about. That man who was talking to you this evening—"

"Mr Hartwell is his name and I suggest you use his name rather than 'that man'."

"Alright then, Mr Hartwell wasn't just talking to you for your brother's benefit; he was doing it for his own benefit. Mr Hartwell clearly found you attractive and took an interest in you and wanted you to know."

"Don't be ridiculous, Duke Cravendish. No man in their right mind could look at me and think I'm attractive."

"So are you saying I'm not in my right mind? Because, Mary, I will let you into a secret. I was attracted to you the first moment I set eyes upon you in the library at Lord and Lady Peacock's estate."

"I think you lie, Duke Cravendish. Convincingly well, I might add, but still a lie."

"Mary, I do believe you are the most stubborn woman I've ever had the pleasure of knowing. If you don't believe what I'm telling you then I'll just have to show you," said Duke Cravendish as he pulled Mary close and kissed her.

Duke Cravendish kissed her in such a way that Mary felt that her knees would buckle underneath her as she swayed in his arms.

"I take it I've made my point. Is it clear to you now? Though I must say, you were quite responsive," said Duke Cravendish.

"You made it perfectly clear that you desire me," responded Mary.

"Well, in that case, with your reasoning you must desire me too," said Duke Cravendish.

With that, Duke Cravendish adjusted his attire and left the room, leaving Mary to slump over the lounger that was behind her. Mary contemplated the nerve of Duke

Cravendish. How could she be so foolish again to let Duke Cravendish kiss her? And why was she left falling apart?

"Richard, why are you eavesdropping from the landing? Can't you see it's a private matter between them?" said Marinea.

"Sorry, my dear. I've never seen a woman try to put Dylan in his place before. Looks like he's finally found a woman who he can't charm his way around," replied Richard.

"Well, Mary is usually very guarded. Clearly Dylan affects her in some way. Quick, come away before they spot us eavesdropping."

The next night they were attending a ball held by some acquaintances of Mr and Mrs Miller. Mary had been dreading the event all day, Marinea had picked out a gown for Mary and helped arrange her hairstyle.

"Mary, relax, would you? Nobody's going to know you there. It will all be fine," said Marinea.

Once they were there, Mary found herself relaxing and for once enjoying being at a ball.

"Being away from your mother is clearly making you more relaxed, Mary," said Marinea.

"Oh, Marinea, the feeling of not being watched is certainly making me feel more relaxed," replied Mary.

"Mary, will you do me the honour of a dance with me?" asked Mr Miller.

"Oh, Mr Miller," said Mary wearily, not sure if she should accept or not.

"Come have a dance with me and I will introduce you to the crowd of Bath afterwards," said Mr Miller.

Mary enjoyed her dance with Mr Miller and after it, she was even asked to dance with a few other gentlemen as well.

"Well, hello again, Miss Mary," said Mr Hartwell.

"Mr Hartwell, I didn't know you were here in attendance tonight."

"Are you disappointed to see me, Miss Mary?"

"No, not at all, Mr Hartwell."

"I see you are the belle of tonight's ball."

"I wouldn't say that, Mr Hartwell."

"Well, I haven't seen you without a dance partner all evening. I was hoping you would save a dance for me."

"Well then, Mr Hartwell, you're in luck. I am free for the next dance."

While Mary was enjoying herself on the dance floor, Duke Cravendish was stood on the sidelines, watching.

"Well, hello again, Cravendish. I wouldn't expect to see you here at a ball," said Madam Boulagise.

"I'm a guest of Mr and Mrs Millers'; it would be rude not to attend," replied Dylan.

"So tell me, does it have anything to do with the young lady you were with at the opera last night? My, I can certainly see your little companion – Miss Mary, I believe her name is – getting a lot of attention here at tonight's ball," said Madam Boulagise.

"What can I do for you, Madam Boulagise?" asked Dylan.

"I would like you to introduce me to her. I do believe Miss Mary and I could become close acquaintances," replied Madam Boulagise.

"I seriously doubt that, Madam Boulagise."

"So, does that mean I can't count on you to introduce me to Miss Mary because you want to keep her all to yourself? Come, Cravendish, I've been watching you watching her all evening, and I'm just curious as to what she's done to you or what she's doing to you to hold your attention. Or maybe I'll ask her myself as I do believe she's heading in this direction."

Duke Cravendish then swept off to intercept Mary before she could reach Madam Boulagise. Mary was just thanking Mr Hartwell for the dance when Duke Cravendish cut in.

"I do believe you promised the next dance to me, Miss Mary," said Duke Cravendish.

"Of course. I'm sorry, Mr Hartwell. Hopefully we can carry on our conversation later," said Mary.

"Of course. Miss Mary, Mr Dylan, until later," said Mr Hartwell.

Madam Boulagise approached the gentleman who had just partnered Miss Mary. She hadn't caught his name but she had heard the gentleman call Cravendish 'Mr Dylan'.

"Excuse me, kind sir," said Madam Boulagise.

"Madam Boulagise, isn't it? I saw your performance last night. You were amazing," said Mr Hartwell.

"Yes, thank you. That gentleman now dancing with Miss Mary, did I hear you call him Mr Dylan?"

"Yes, that's right. Is that not his name? Miss Mary introduced me to him last night as Mr Dylan," said Mr Hartwell, puzzled.

"Oh, his name's Dylan alright, just not his surname," replied Madam Boulagise.

"Oh, I wonder why Miss Mary introduced him to me as Mr Dylan."

"Probably due to the fact that the gentleman wants to keep his surname a secret."

"So tell me, Madam Boulagise, what is the gentleman's surname?"

Madam Boulagise gave a sly smile before answering.

"The gentleman is actually known as Captain Cravendish, also now known as Duke Cravendish."

"Well, I'm sure Miss Mary wasn't aware of his surname when she introduced us."

"Are you quite sure of that?" asked Madam Boulagise slyly.

Meanwhile Dylan was on the dance floor with Mary and it was now his turn to start the conversation.

"Well, Mary, you do seem to have attracted a certain number of admirers in your short time here in Bath. I noticed you and Mr Hartwell were deep in conversation," said Duke Cravendish.

"Well, we have a lot in common. Not only is he a dear friend of my brother William, we even have a lot of interests in common. Mr Hartwell is a music lover and also a keen reader like myself, though I would have got to know him better if you hadn't interrupted. Do you have a problem with Mr Hartwell, Duke Cravendish?" asked Mary, wondering why Duke Cravendish had cut in when she was talking to Mr Hartwell.

"No, not at all, Mary, just concerned that you're going to break the poor man's heart," said Duke Cravendish.

"Are you trying to say I'm heartless? Because if the boot fits, Duke Cravendish, I suggest you look at your own life before casting aspersions on mine," replied Mary.

"Meaning?" said Dylan.

"You've left a string of broken hearts behind you, have you not, Duke Cravendish? Now, if you'll excuse me, I wish to talk to Madam Boulagise because I see she is here tonight. And she is clearly enjoying her conversation with Mr Hartwell, so if you won't introduce us then Mr Hartwell will," said Mary.

As Mary walked off the dance floor to see Mr Hartwell, Duke Cravendish followed after her.

"Madam Boulagise, it is an honour to meet you in person. We saw your performance last night. Do you get much free time in-between performances?" asked Mary.

"Not as much as I would like. You are Miss Mary Barker, I believe? Of course, you know Mr Hartwell. I must say, you and Cravendish do make a lovely partnership out there on the dance floor," said Madam Boulagise.

"Thank you, Madam Boulagise," said Mary, not realising that Madam Boulagise had used Duke Cravendish's surname to address him.

"So, your name is not Mr Dylan then?" said Mr Hartwell to Duke Cravendish.

"No. I'm sorry for the misunderstanding, Mr Hartwell, but you'll have to ask Miss Mary why she misled you regarding my surname. So tell us, Miss Mary, why did you mislead poor Mr Hartwell regarding my surname?" said Duke Cravendish.

"Well, it was because I didn't want you to judge Duke Cravendish based on what you've heard of his reputation before getting to know him. I wouldn't discard a book just because I didn't like how its title sounded," said Mary, defending the reason why she had misled Mr Hartwell regarding Duke Cravendish.

"Well, Miss Mary, I hear you're a great performer on the piano. You should call around one day, when I don't have a performance on that is, and we could do a duet together – I would most like to hear you play," said Madam Boulagise.

"Well, in that case I would be honoured, Madam Boulagise," replied Mary.

"Miss Mary is being polite, Madam Boulagise. I believe she has other obligations to attend to first," said Duke Cravendish.

"Well, I hope you can extend your time here in Bath. I'll speak to Mrs Miller myself and arrange it, Miss Mary, if that's what it takes. Well, if you'll excuse me, I've a midnight show; I must go and get myself ready. Miss Mary, keep a lookout for my invitation," said Madam Boulagise.

"I very much look forward to it, Madam Boulagise. Mr Hartwell, won't you favour a lady with another dance?"

"Miss Mary, I would be honoured to do so."

While they are on the dance floor Mr Hartwell is the one to first ask a question.

Do I take it you don't want word to get back to William that Duke Cravendish is here in Bath?" asked Mr Hartwell.

"That's one thing. I also wanted to ask, what is your impression of Madam Boulagise?" asked Mary.

"Well, I'm probably not the best person to ask. I really don't know that much about her, only that she's French and tours a lot; that is all I know I'm afraid. Why are you asking? I thought you didn't judge a book by its title."

"I don't. I'm just curious about what you think of Madam Boulagise."

"Or is there another reason why you're asking?"

"You know my brother William. What do you think he

would tell me about making an acquaintance with Madam Boulagise?"

"I would say he would disapprove and tell you to think of your reputation."

"Well, I wasn't expecting William and Duke Cravendish to agree on anything, so what's William got against Madam Boulagise do you think?"

"Miss Mary, if you want the truth, it's all to do with the French style of life."

"Your point being?"

"The French are more open and free with affairs of the heart."

"So, you are saying having a friendship with a French lady may make people think I live the French lifestyle as well?"

Later that night, back at the Millers' house, the gentlemen departed to the billiard room for drinks while Marinea and Mary went into the library to talk.

"Mary, I think that's the first time in my life that I've seen you enjoying yourself at a ball. You did enjoy yourself, didn't you? You weren't faking enjoying yourself for my benefit?" asked Marinea.

"Oh, Marinea, I truly did have a wonderful time and I'm loving my time here in Bath and enjoying the pleasures that Bath brings. Madam Boulagise was there tonight. She's invited me to take tea with her while I'm in town," replied Mary.

"How wonderful, Mary, and you have Mr Hartwell's visits to look forward to as well."

"Dylan, I saw Madam Boulagise talking with Miss

Mary. I hope you warned Miss Mary to be careful around Madam Boulagise," said Richard.

"I tried to warn her, Richard, but Miss Mary, she has a stubborn streak a mile wide. Don't worry, Richard, I plan on gatecrashing Mary's tea with Madam Boulagise and making sure Madam Boulagise is on her best behaviour. Miss Mary is a country girl who likes to see the best in everybody and I can just see Madam Boulagise doing something to her," said Dylan.

"You think she might compromise her in some way?" asked Richard.

"I wouldn't put anything past her, Richard."

"Does Madam Boulagise have it in for you?"

"I suppose she could do as we were lovers in the past from time to time."

"And she wants you to carry on being lovers?"

"Yes, I think so. She saw me with Miss Mary and was asking questions about her."

"You think she could be jealous?"

"I'm not sure, though I do have my concerns over the whole situation. I'll tell you of my concerns, Richard, and we will both have to make sure we keep an eye on the situation."

Chapter Sixteen

It was a nice sunny spring day and a tour of Bath's gardens and parks was the agenda for the morning.

"So are the gardens and parks usually busy, Marinea?" asked Mary.

"They can be; they're a popular meeting place."

"So it's where people gather to exchange gossip."

"People here refer to it as 'knowledge gathering'. Couples usually take a tour of the gardens in carriages. I'm sure Mr Hartwell is planning on inviting you on a carriage ride around the park when he comes to call on you. I will write to Mrs Barker and tell her you've attracted a suitor and ask for you not to leave Bath too soon," said Marinea.

"I'm sure Mother will be over the moon to hear such delightful news. May I ask you, Marinea, what's your take on Madam Boulagise?" asked Mary. "I've been warned to stay clear of her but the only reason I've been given is that she's French."

"Do you want me to ask Richard his opinion on Madam Boulagise?" asked Marinea.

"No, he will know why you're asking and just say what Duke Cravendish tells him to say."

"What if I ask about Duke Cravendish and his relationship with Madam Boulagise?" asked Marinea.

"That could work, Marinea, but we need to try and work it into a conversation so it seems natural."

"Come on, Mary. I want to take you to my dressmaker and get a dress made for you to remind you of your time here in Bath."

They returned to the house a few hours later. Godfrey, Mr and Mrs Miller's butler, was waiting for them.

"Welcome back, Mrs Miller, Miss Mary. A gentleman called round earlier when you were out. He left his calling card and said he would call around again tomorrow if you are free, Miss Mary."

"It's from Mr Hartwell, Marinea," said Mary.

"My, Mr Hartwell is certainly keen to call upon you, Mary," said Marinea.

"Are the gentlemen back yet, Godfrey?" asked Marinea.

"No, I believe the gentlemen are still out, but the master said they would be back before dinner," said Godfrey.

Dinner was a quiet affair with just the four of them round the table.

"So, Duke Cravendish, Richard tells me that in your former life you were a sea captain. Can you tell us some tales of being at sea?" said Marinea.

"Please call me Dylan. And that's true, I have seen many places and visited lots of different countries, trading in goods all around different islands."

"So have you experienced much of Europe in your travels?"

"I've called in at many French ports in my time."

"Any favourite city you have a preference for?"

"I have seen many wonderful places but nothing beats the sense of being home."

"Have you ever managed to see inland France at all? I've always wanted to visit Paris myself."

"Of course, Paris being the height of fashion, I may have ventured into Paris on occasions."

"I believe the women dress in much fancier clothes than in England."

"Yes, fancier maybe, but with less material in the clothes."

"Do the women there have the freedom to do as they please? One has heard gossip of what French women are like but one does not want to say in public."

"Yes, I suppose that's true. Paris is the city of lovers."

"So the women of Paris take lovers like men?"

"Some do like to take lovers; some more than one."

"Like those that take part in performance art, like Madam Boulagise?" said Mary.

"Yes, Mary, Madam Boulagise has been known for taking lovers."

"Of course. So if a single female called around, people could get the wrong idea, but if two ladies called around that would be alright? Then Marinea will accompany me wherever I go. If you excuse me, I wish to retire for the evening," said Mary as she got up from the table to return to her room.

"Of course, Miss Mary, we will see you at breakfast," said Mr Miller.

"Good morning, Mary. I hope you slept well. The

gentlemen have already gone out for the day," said Marinea.

"Marinea, what do you have planned for us today?"

"Well, you must remember that Mr Hartwell is to call upon you today."

"Oh yes, I remember. I wonder what he wants to see us about."

"Ladies, a Mr Hartwell is here to see you," said Godfrey.

"Very good, Godfrey, you may send him through," replied Marinea.

"Good morning, Mrs Miller, Miss Mary. I was wondering if you would accompany me on a ride around Bath? If you are free, that is," said Mr Hartwell eagerly.

"Yes, I'm free, but I'm afraid Marinea here is acting as my chaperone so I hope you don't mind if Marinea accompanies us," replied Mary.

"Not at all. How can I complain? Having two beautiful women by my side will be a bonus. I was hoping you might like to see the Parade Gardens. It gives beautiful views of the city. That is, if Mrs Miller hasn't shown you the view already," said Mr Hartwell.

"That sounds lovely, Mr Hartwell; that is somewhere we haven't been yet. I remember Richard took me there on our first outing around Bath. It's quite a romantic spot. Lots of lovely scenery to see too," said Marinea.

"Well, it does sound lovely, to look down at Bath and to pick out the different districts," said Mary.

"I wrote to William, Miss Mary, and told him of us meeting, and I also followed your wishes by not mentioning a certain gentleman who is in town. Though I disagree with deceiving him," said Mr Hartwell.

"Thank you, Mr Hartwell, I appreciate you doing that for me, though I don't believe I'm deceiving William. I'm just not informing him of everything," said Mary.

"Please allow me to help you ladies into the carriage. So how is everything going for you here in Bath? Are you enjoying yourself?"

"Oh, very much so. Marinea here has done an amazing job of showing me the delights. We've been to the theatre and to a ball or two, as well as having a small dinner party."

"Well, it wasn't a dinner party per se as there was only the four of us there, Mary. However, if we were to hold a dinner party, you would certainly be invited, Mr Hartwell."

"Well, I thank you for the future invite, Mrs Miller. This is Pulteney Bridge we are crossing now and we will arrive in Parade Gardens shortly. From our start point here we can see Bath Abbey, and further round we get to see the Roman Baths," said Mr Hartwell, sharing his knowledge of Bath.

"It's certainly an amazing view you get of Bath from up here, Mr Hartwell," said Mary as she was taking in all of the sites.

"May I call on you again later this week, Miss Mary?" said Mr Hartwell when they got back to the Millers' house.

"Oh yes, of course, Mr Hartwell. We look forward to it," replied Mary.

"Then I will thank you for today and I will look forward to our next outing together," said Mr Hartwell as he bid the ladies goodbye.

"Ladies, how was your morning ride with Mr Hartwell? A letter came for you whilst you were out," said Godfrey.

"Thank you, Godfrey. We had a lovely time," said Marinea.

"Oh my, it's from Madam Boulagise. She's invited us around for tea tomorrow afternoon, just after lunch. Are we able to attend?" asked Mary.

"I believe I've got a women's liberation meeting tomorrow morning, but we should be free later in the day. Oh, I forgot, Mr Miller and I will be out tomorrow night at a dinner party. We told them we had guests but some people just don't take no for an answer," said Marinea.

"Sounds like my mother; she will not stop until people agree with what she's saying," said Mary.

"Will you be alright here with Duke Cravendish?" asked Marinea with concern for her friend.

"Marinea, everything will be fine. We're not likely to kill one another," replied Mary.

"I'm just concerned that you both have a passionate temperament, that's all," said Marinea.

"I'm sure Duke Cravendish and I can manage to be civil to each other for one evening."

"So, you've a dinner party to go to tomorrow night then, Richard?" said Dylan.

"Yes, you'll be alone with Miss Mary, so check your behaviour," said Richard.

"I'm sure Miss Mary and I can be civil to one another without other people being around to chaperone us."

"Have you had any more news from Skip about how your ship's doing?"

"No. I should head to Bristol and find out what's going on, though."

"But something or someone is holding you back here in Bath. Are you making plans to leave Bath in the next few days?"

"I'll be arranging to leave soon. I thank you, Richard, for your hospitality in inviting me to stay."

The next morning Mary went with Marinea to attend her women's liberation meeting which was being held by a Miss Fisher.

"Morning, everyone. I would like to introduce you to my friend all the way from Derbyshire, Miss Mary Barker," said Marinea.

"Well, it's always nice to have new faces. Won't you come and sit down? We are just about to start today's meeting. Let me introduce you to everybody. My name's Miss Doris Fisher and this is Mrs Georgina Dunn, Mrs Philippa Brooks and Mrs Penelope Reed. Miss Mary, it's good to meet an old friend of Marinea's. How are you finding Bath? I believe you have a great interest in women's rights so Marinea tells us, so what do you think should be changed in this country?" asked Doris Fisher, who was curious to hear what Mary thought.

"Well, I think it would be a massive improvement if women were given the same rights as our male counterparts. For example, is a woman actually really free? First she belongs to her father; then she is married and regarded as her husband's property, thereby giving the aforementioned husband control of the lady's fortune. I, for one, believe a female should be given the right to do with her fortune as she pleases, and do what she wants to do without people judging her for her beliefs," said Mary.

"You're quite right, Mary. That's why I chose not to marry. I would rather control my own money than give a man control of my fortune," replied Doris Fisher.

"My, you certainly do have an opinion on women's rights, Miss Mary," replied Penelope Reed who was only really there for social reasons.

"As you can see Mary has quite a strong opinion on women's rights," said Marinea.

"So we can see," replied Philippa Brooks who wasn't as fully committed to women's rights as some of the others.

"Marinea, I do believe I'll wait outside until your meeting is finished. I believe I may have offended some of the ladies here with my comments," said Mary.

"Mary, you don't have to leave," said Marinea.

"I think it's best if I do. Thank you for having me. You have a lovely home," said Mary.

"I must say, Marinea, your friend is certainly vocal in her opinions. The next thing you know, your friend Mary will be wanting a woman to run the country. Can you imagine that?" said Penelope Reed.

"I don't see what the problem would be with a woman running the country. I mean, we are just as capable as our male counterparts in regards to running things, are we not? After all, we already run our own households," replied Marinea.

"Yes, thank you for that, Marinea. But we can't change the country overnight, can we?" said Georgina Dunn.

"Now ladies I know we can get overly passionate regarding our opinions; may I suggest we all calm down and have some tea?" said Doris Fisher.

The meeting carried on for another half an hour with

the ladies debating which concerns should be tackled first; then Georgina Dunn spoke again.

"Now, is there any other business that anyone would like to bring up or shall we call it a day?" replied Georgina Dunn.

As most of the ladies gathered up their cloaks to prepare to leave, Doris Fisher kept Marinea behind to tell her something.

"I must say, Marinea, I for one was most impressed with your friend Mary. It's a shame there aren't more women out there like her," said Doris Fisher.

"Thank you, Doris, though I don't think some of the others would agree with you."

When Marinea came out of the meeting, she looked for Mary but couldn't see her.

"I'm sorry, sir, you haven't seen the companion I was with earlier, have you?" Marinea asked the footman.

"Mrs Miller, she left a few moments ago. She asked me to give you this note and said you would understand."

Marinea read the note the footman had just handed to her.

"Thank you."

Mary, you headstrong, foolish girl, thought Marinea as she caught a carriage home to Mr Miller and Duke Cravendish.

"Marinea, is everything alright? Where's Miss Mary?" asked Richard.

"She slipped away?" asked Duke Cravendish.

"She did. She's gone to visit Madam Boulagise. She left me this note," said Marinea as she showed the note to Richard and Dylan, and with that Dylan got up to leave the room.

"Dylan, where are going?" asked Richard.

"To rescue Miss Mary before she gets into any trouble," replied Dylan as he hurried out of the house.

Chapter Seventeen

"Miss Mary Barker is here to see you, Madam Boulagise," said the servant who was showing Mary in.

"Mary, come in, please. I'm so glad you could come and see me before I have to depart Bath. Come, let me introduce you to Anton," said Madam Boulagise.

"Anton is your musician, right? Oh, I do hope I haven't interrupted your practice," said Mary with concern. She knew from personal experience how annoying it was when your performance was interrupted even if you were only practising.

"Not at all, we have just finished," said Madam Boulagise.

"It's a pleasure to meet you, Miss Mary; however, I shall leave you ladies to it," said Anton as he got up from where he had been sitting at the piano.

Anton left the room, kissing both ladies on both cheeks.

"You'll have to forgive Anton, Mary, he's Italian and not used to the English way of greeting or bidding farewell," said Madam Boulagise.

"Please come sit. So you are Miss Mary Barker. I believe I have had the pleasure of meeting one of your sisters once."

"Oh my! Which sister might that be? I do have four of them, after all," enquired Mary.

"Oh yes, of course you do. It was when I was down in Brighton. I met your sister... Linda, is it? Your youngest sister, I believe."

"Yes, Linda is my younger sister. But please forgive her; she's not like the rest of my sisters. She is what my father refers to as the black sheep of the family."

"Oh. Well, when I met Linda, I thought she could have some French blood in her, but are the rest of you truly British then? I thought maybe you yourself might have had some French blood as well. I hear you wish to be independent and have no need of a husband."

"I'm sorry to disappoint you, Madam Boulagise, but I lack the French sensuality."

"Of course, that explains it all."

"I'm sorry, Madam Boulagise, I don't understand your meaning."

"Dylan Cravendish's interest in you has not wavered and I was wondering why. Now I know. He has not had you yet, not plucked you, so to speak."

"Excuse me, Madam Boulagise?"

"The man clearly wants you, yet you turn him down. That explains why he didn't take me up on my offer."

"I'm sorry, Madam Boulagise?"

"May I be blunt? Why don't you want to have Dylan Cravendish as a lover? I mean, if you're worried of people finding out, I can assure you that discretion is his middle name, and he is one of the best I've ever had. You've never been tempted to think of Dylan Cravendish in that way? Or you have, and that's why when talking about him you refer to him by his title, to avoid getting personal?"

"Thank you for that, Madam Boulagise, but I'm not looking to have a lover."

"Well, in that case, how about we just perform together so then you haven't had a wasted trip and I haven't wasted an afternoon?" said Madam Boulagise, who was now irritated by Mary.

"Miss Mary, are you alright?" asked Duke Cravendish with concern in his voice.

"Dylan Cravendish! My, we didn't know you were here. Did you slip in through the servants' entrance?" asked Madam Boulagise.

"Mrs Miller was concerned about Miss Mary. I was sent to make sure she was alright and see her safely back to the Millers' house," said Duke Cravendish.

"Oh, Miss Mary, I did enjoy our conversation. And keep in mind what I said, should you ever change your mind regarding the matters we discussed," said Madam Boulagise.

"Well, I thank you for your time, Madam Boulagise, and wish you all the best on your tour," said Mary.

Then Duke Cravendish escorted Mary out of the house and proceeded to see her back to the Millers' house.

"Marinea was concerned when you disappeared off on your own to see Madam Boulagise after everybody advised you to stay clear of her. What did she want to see you about anyway?" asked Duke Cravendish.

"She met Linda in Brighton and wanted to know if I was like Linda. Are you happy now, Duke Cravendish?

You were right about why she wanted to see me, and I was wrong. Now we should let the matter rest if we are to have a civil dinner together. Marinea told me earlier that her and Richard are being forced to attend a dinner party tonight that they can't get out of," said Mary.

"Of course, I'm sure we can both manage that. Come along now, I'll see you safely back to Marinea," said Duke Cravendish.

They then arrived back at the Millers' house, upon hearing their voices Marinea came running out into the hallway.

"Mary, are you alright? I was concerned when the footman handed me your note and told me you had left already.; I told you I would accompany you to see Madam Boulagise," said Marinea.

"I know, I'm sorry, Marinea. I didn't know how long you would be and I didn't want to miss meeting Madam Boulagise. Please forgive me, Marinea," said Mary.

"Oh, Mary, I was just concerned about your welfare. However, I'm pleased everything's alright and we got to see you before we have to leave for this dinner party," said Marinea as she was heading upstairs.

Mary then went upstairs with Marinea so they could finish talking in Marinea's private dressing room.

"Come help me change. How about you tell me what you think of the outfit I have picked out for tonight? And tell me what Madam Boulagise wanted to see you about, Mary."

"Oh, Madam Boulagise only wanted to meet me because she met Linda in Brighton and she thought I was like Linda."

"Oh, Mary, I'm so sorry it was a disappointment for you."

"She was under the impression that Duke Cravendish was trying to pursue me as a lover and decided to tell me about her experience of having Duke Cravendish as a lover."

"So, do you feel anything for Duke Cravendish, Mary?" asked Marinea.

"I hardly know the man, Marinea, and I'm certainly not looking for a lover," replied Mary.

"I sense a 'but' coming, Mary. Tell me what you're not telling me," said Marinea.

"When Duke Cravendish kisses me, it makes me go weak at the knees."

"Duke Cravendish kissed you when? And it sounds like more than once?" said Marinea, who was shocked by what she was hearing.

"Well, the first time was during a ball out in the garden – we were talking and I heard someone coming, as I didn't want to be seen with Duke Cravendish I pulled him into the hedge maze; then he just kissed my wrist. Then here the other night, after the opera, was when he kissed me properly, and I just melted, though I refuse to be won over by his charms. It was an attempt, no doubt, to end our conversation, but I know what he is and I'm not going to be bowled over by a kiss. Anyway, he seemed most interested in Helena Valentine when we first met," said Mary.

"Helena Valentine? What's she got to do with anything?" asked Marinea.

"She was with Duke Cravendish when I first met him."

"I thought you met Duke Cravendish at Lady Beatrice's house?" asked Marinea, puzzled.

"No, I lied about that, though I did see Duke Cravendish at Lady Beatrice's house, just not when we first met. The first time I met Duke Cravendish was in Lord and Lady Peacock's library during a ball, and the pair of them were all over each other," said Mary.

"I thought Dylan would have better taste than to get involved with Helena Valentine. You know I've never liked her; I've always thought she thinks she is better than everyone else. Oh, Mary, I'm so sorry you had to experience that moment," said Marinea.

"Don't be, Marinea. It's made me all the wiser of Duke Cravendish's motives," replied Mary.

"So, what happened when you got there? Was Madam Boulagise's partner, Anton the pianist, there?" asked Richard.

"No, thankfully not. It was just Mary and Madam Boulagise who were there but there was certainly tension in the air; something had clearly happened between them."

"Well, I'm just glad you got Mary out of there safely."

Chapter Eighteen

Mr and Mrs Miller departed for their dinner party, leaving Mary and Duke Cravendish to have dinner together.

"Bath seems to be agreeing with you, Mary," said Duke Cravendish.

"I suppose it helps to not be judged against my sisters, their beauty or their demeanour," replied Mary.

"I've never judged you against your sisters; besides I've only met three of them, and I've never found you plain either. I believe I said as much when we first met," said Duke Cravendish. "Come, teach me how to play, Mary. My Aunt Beatrice always wanted me to learn to play – 'increase my talents', she would say – but it never happened."

"Well, we better start with something easy to begin with. You know the key notes, right? Now, you place your hands here for high notes and your other hand here for the lower notes. Alright, how about we try to duet this one together? Just follow my movements. Come, relax your hands like so," instructed Mary.

Taking Duke Cravendish's hands in hers, Mary felt the

roughness of a man who worked with his hands. They were clearly sharing a moment together.

"Mary."

Duke Cravendish turned around to look at Mary, their hands still intertwined.

"Mary, I—"

Duke Cravendish was then interrupted by the sound of laughter coming from just outside of the room. Mary jumped as if she had just been caught doing something that she shouldn't have been doing.

"Mary, Dylan, we are back. I hope everything's been alright between the two of you? We left early, telling them we had guests to rush back and attend to. What's going on in here?"

"Duke Cravendish asked me to teach him how to play the piano. I was giving him a lesson on hand placement."

"Really, Dylan? I never knew you had an interest in learning the piano before," said Richard.

"People can change, Richard," replied Dylan.

"You're back early. How was the dinner party, Marinea?" asked Mary.

"Oh, it was a bit dull really. We were pleased we had an excuse to leave early, to be honest," said Marinea.

"So, what are you two going to play for us to hear?" said Richard.

Mary and Duke Cravendish played a short piece of music together.

"Maybe you should stick to singing rather than playing. You can't be good at everything, Dylan," said Richard.

"Ignore my husband, Dylan. He's just jealous as he has no talent with music," said Marinea.

"Marinea's just being polite," said Richard.

"No, I'm stating a fact. Not everyone can have Mary's natural talent for playing," said Marinea.

"Alright, Mary, tell us how you think Dylan played," asked Mr Miller.

"Well, for a first-time player of the piano, I believe Duke Cravendish picked it up really easily."

"Dylan's always had that talent of picking things up easily," remarked Mr Miller.

Marinea shot her husband a look of disapproval at what he had just said.

"My, look at the time! I think it's about time we called it a night," said Marinea.

Upstairs in their bedroom, Mr and Mrs Miller were talking.

"Richard, why did you have to say that Dylan's always had the ability to pick things up easily?"

"It's the truth. Ever since we were at school, Dylan's always been able to pick things up easily."

"Did you not think how that might have sounded to Mary?" said Marinea.

"No, why should I have?" asked Richard.

"Could you not sense that something was happening between the two of them? Now you saying what you did has probably ruined everything," said Marinea.

Chapter Nineteen

It was the middle of the night when Mary was awakened by the sounds of someone having a nightmare. Mary knew she would never forgive herself if she didn't try to help someone awake from a nightmare. She lit the candle on the bedside table and made her way down the hallway to where the sounds were coming from. She discovered the sounds were coming from Duke Cravendish's room and hesitated before entering. When she opened the door, she saw Duke Cravendish gripped by a nightmare. Mary placed the candle down on the bedside table. She moved over to the bed and began to shake Duke Cravendish in the hopes of wakening him from the nightmare, but with no success. So Mary changed her plan to doing what she did with her nieces and nephews when they had nightmares. Mary called out his name in sweet tones.

"Dylan, wake up, it's alright," said Mary.

Mary repeated it over and over. Dylan heard the voice calling out to him, the sweet voice of Mary calling out his first name. He was clearly dreaming.

"Oh Mary, my sweet Mary, how I've longed for you," said Dylan in a sleepy voice.

Mary felt herself being grabbed and rolled over. She found herself pinned under Duke Cravendish's body. Mary pinched him in order to wake him up. Dylan woke suddenly to discover Mary was under him.

"Mary, what the hell are you doing in here?" asked Dylan angrily.

"You were having a nightmare. I was trying to wake you up, then you grabbed me and rolled me over," said Mary, trying to explain herself.

Dylan wanted to climb out of bed to have this conversation, then he realised that wouldn't be a good idea as he slept in the nude.

"Mary, did you even think what could happen when you walked into my room or if anybody saw you come in here? Damn it, Mary, don't you think? Anything could have happened to you."

"Nothing did happen. It's not the first time I've gone into someone's room when they're having a nightmare."

"That's it, Mary, I'm going to make sure you stay in your own room."

Dylan, not caring that he was naked, now climbed out of bed, pushed Mary against the bedroom door and kissed her. Mary responded to his kiss, deepening it.

"Mary, you need to leave right now before something happens between us."

Mary rushed out of the room, out into the corridor and back to her room. How was it that every time she was alone with Duke Cravendish, they ended up kissing? The man certainly knew how to get under Mary's skin.

What the hell had Mary been thinking, slipping into his room like that? Who cared that he was having a nightmare?

She shouldn't have intervened. What if he hadn't awoken when he had? Anything could have happened to her, and he knew he could never forgive himself if it did. He only hoped that he had scared some sense into her.

The following morning, the air was filled with silence around the breakfast table.

"You wrote to Skip to tell him you were on your way to check up on things? Let's hope he's getting everything sorted out then," said Richard.

"Are you leaving already, Dylan?" asked Marinea.

"Sadly I am, Marinea. I wish to thank you and Richard for all you've done for me; however, I need to carry on my journey to Bristol."

"You're not heading back to Cattleton, then?" asked Mary.

"No, not yet, Mary. I need to carry out some unfinished business in Bristol, then, hopefully, once everything's sorted out I will return to Cattleton. I have a lot of faith and trust in Hugh so I know he will have everything running smoothly at the Cravendish estate during my absence," said Duke Cravendish.

"Right. Well, if you'll excuse us, ladies, we have business to attend to before Dylan departs tomorrow," said Mr Miller as they both left the room.

"Mary, I'm sorry to do this to you, but I have to run an errand that I totally forgot about. Are you alright here on your own?" asked Marinea.

"Everything will be fine, Marinea," said Mary.

"Godfrey's here if anything happens in my absence."

Chapter Twenty

"Miss Mary, there is a visitor here to see you. I don't know if I should invite him in or not as, you see, Mrs Miller gave me orders not to let anyone untoward in," said Godfrey.

"Well, who is it that wishes to call upon me?" asked Mary.

"A Mr John Hartwell, Miss Mary," said Godfrey.

"I know Mr Hartwell, we've met on quite a few occasions. You can let him in, Godfrey," replied Mary.

"Very good, Miss Mary, I shall send him through straight away."

"Thank you, Godfrey."

"Miss Mary, it's good to see you again. I'm sorry if I've called in at a bad time," said Mr Hartwell.

"Oh no, not at all. Godfrey was just concerned about letting you in as Mrs Miller has popped out, but she will be back shortly," said Mary.

"That sounds very wise of him. It's always good to be curious of letting people in, especially when the owners aren't home. However, it was you I wanted to talk to."

"Oh right. Shall I ring for some tea, Mr Hartwell?" said Mary.

"No, I'm quite alright unless you wish to have some," replied Mr Hartwell.

"Mr Hartwell, please take a seat, you're making me nervous. Was there something I could do for you?"

"I'm sorry. I'm making a bumbling fool of myself. I wished to have a private word with you, if that's alright."

"Of course, Mr Hartwell."

"Please call me John, Mary, 'Mr Hartwell' seems too formal."

"Forgive me, I've never got used to calling a gentleman by his given name before. Go on, Mr Hartwell, ask me what you came here to ask me."

"Well, Mary, as you know, your brother William is a good friend of mine and, well, we're kind of like brothers, and I hope maybe one day I will be able to call him my brother."

"Oh, Mr Hartwell."

"Mary, please let me finish my asking before you give me your answer."

"Alright, Mr Hartwell, finish asking your question."

"Even before I met you, Mary, I knew you were the one who would capture my heart and soul from how William described you to me. And then we finally met and I still felt that way…"

Then Mary kissed Mr Hartwell to see if it was possible for him to be right, but nothing happened. Mary felt nothing.

"Well, I was not expecting that until after I had asked and you had given me your answer," said Mr Hartwell.

"Oh, Mr Hartwell, please forgive me. I shouldn't have led you on. I wanted to know if I could feel that way about you and when I kissed you a moment ago, I got my answer. I'm sorry, Mr Hartwell, but I don't feel the same way about you and I would hate for you to give love but not to have it given back. I know you and William are close friends and I hope my answer doesn't affect your friendship with William."

"Not at all, Miss Mary, I accept your honesty in such matters. However, I think it's best if I leave now," said Mr Hartwell, getting up to leave just as Marinea returned.

"I'm sorry, Mrs Miller. Thank you and goodbye. Miss Mary, I will pass on your best wishes to William when I return to Southampton," said Mr Hartwell as he left the room and the house.

"Mary, is everything alright? What's happened between you and Mr Hartwell to make him leave so suddenly?" asked Marinea, who had just arrived as Mr Hartwell was leaving.

"He didn't like the answer he received to his question," replied Mary.

"Oh, I see. Mr Hartwell proposed to you then," said Marinea.

"Mr Hartwell told me he believed us to be an ideal fit, and he even said he knew from the way William described me that I was his heart and soul."

"But you didn't feel like that then, Mary?"

"No, I like Mr Hartwell's company and all that but when I kissed him, I felt nothing. So, I told him as much. Why give your love away when your love can't be returned?"

"You kissed him! Well, at least he asked you here and

not in Cattleton; your mother would be trying to get you to go after Mr Hartwell and accept his proposal otherwise. If you had agreed then there would be another miserable married couple. You did the right thing, Mary, you followed your heart and your head. Clearly you are not meant to be the spinster Barker people speak about; maybe you're just waiting for the right proposal to come along."

"What are you saying, Marinea? That I may one day decide that I want a husband?"

"The right one could come along – I'm sure the ideal man is out there for you."

Chapter Twenty-One

"Isn't that John Hartwell, a friend of Miss Mary's brother who we've seen at a few balls over the last week or two? He doesn't look very happy at the moment, does he?" said Richard.

"He looks as drunk as a skunk and he looks like he's leaving," said Dylan.

"Dylan, we've got to make sure he gets back to his lodgings alright; we can't leave him to wander off in his condition, anything could happen to him in that state," said Richard. "Are you alright there, Mr Hartwell? Let us help you back to your lodgings. Things will look brighter tomorrow," said Richard as he and Dylan came to Mr Hartwell's aid.

Mr Hartwell didn't answer; he just swayed on his feet.

They had just got Mr Hartwell to his lodgings when he decided to speak to them for the first time since they had started helping him.

"You know, I hate you right now. I should have followed my instincts and informed William you were here trying to seduce his sister," said Mr Hartwell as he tried to take a swing at Duke Cravendish.

Luckily, Dylan was used to other men trying to take a swing at him, so he easily dodged.

"Hang on, Mr Hartwell, we are trying to help you here," said Richard.

Luckily, a servant came to the door just a moment later and helped Mr Hartwell into his lodgings, giving Mr Miller and Duke Cravendish the opportunity to leave and return back to the Miller household. Marinea was sat alone in the front parlour when Richard walked in alone.

"I don't know what's happened to poor Mr Hartwell, but Dylan and I saw him at the club and the man was as drunk as a skunk. We had to help him back to his lodgings, poor fellow. He even tried to take a swing at Dylan when we were trying to help him," said Richard.

"Oh dear," said Marinea.

"Marinea, I don't like the sound of that 'oh dear'."

"Richard, what I'm about to tell you, you must keep to yourself, alright?"

"Marinea, what is it?" asked Richard, concerned that something was wrong.

"Mr Hartwell called around earlier and proposed to Mary and she turned him down. The man clearly thought Mary would accept his offer – he even had William's blessing to ask her – but Mary turned him down," said Marinea.

"What? So Mr Hartwell blames Dylan for Mary turning him down? That's why he took a swing at him?" asked Richard.

"I don't know, Richard, but don't go reading anything into it."

"So, how's Mary taking things?" asked Richard.

"She was shocked by his proposal but she is now rummaging through your books in the library as we speak. Where's Dylan? I thought he was staying another night," asked Marinea.

"He is. He's gone into the library for some peace," replied Richard.

"Oh no, I hope they don't come to blows," said Marinea.

"Who?"

"Mary and Dylan."

"Why would they come to blows?" asked Richard.

"Oh Richard, do keep up, my dear."

"Mary, I'm sorry to disturb you. I didn't know you were in here," said Duke Cravendish as he entered the room.

"Oh, that's quite alright, Duke Cravendish, I was—"

"Just devouring your way through all of Richard's books, by the looks of things," replied Duke Cravendish.

"Yes. I'm sorry about last night. Reading helps take my mind off things."

"Mr Hartwell, by any chance?" enquired Duke Cravendish.

"What makes you think that, Duke Cravendish?" asked Mary.

"Just a feeling I had... and the fact that Richard and I had to help him back to his lodging."

"Oh dear, I hope he's alright. I never took Mr Hartwell for being a drinker. I guess I didn't know him at all. I suppose it's all my fault and he blames me for his drinking."

"No, I think he blames me. He tried to take a swing at me. And besides, he will get over it and find someone else."

"You know, don't you?"

"I know what, Mary?"

"That Mr Hartwell called around earlier on today and proposed, and that I turned him down."

"I had my suspicions that Mr Hartwell was going to propose to you at some point during your stay here in Bath."

"How could you know of Mr Hartwell's intentions when I did not?"

"Mary, I am a man of the world. After all, you did what was right for you, you have nothing to be ashamed of. Most women would have just accepted, but you followed your heart, Mary."

"But I kissed Mr Hartwell to make sure I was doing the right thing and I felt nothing, but when you kiss me I—"

Then Duke Cravendish kissed her again.

"I'm sorry, Mary, I shouldn't keep doing that. The reason I came in here was that I wanted to find you to say I'm sorry for how I reacted last night. Though your actions were just out of concern for me, you need to know the dangers. If someone saw you entering or exiting my room, it could be very misconstrued. I'm surprised William hasn't instructed you in such matters."

There was a knock at the door before Mary could answer.

"I'm sorry to interrupt, Duke Cravendish, but a parcel has just been dropped off for Miss Mary," said Godfrey.

"I'm not expecting any deliveries, Godfrey," said Mary.

"A gentleman dropped it off just a moment ago."

"A gentleman? What gentleman? Who was it, Godfrey?" asks Duke Cravendish.

"I don't know, sir, he didn't give me a name, just handed

over the package and asked it to be given to Miss Mary straight away," said Godfrey.

"It wasn't Mr Hartwell as Godfrey has met Mr Hartwell," said Mary.

"Well, thank you, Godfrey. I will have a look to see if they left a note," said Mary.

Mary opened the package to unravel a gown, which was wrapped up in a lot of paper.

"This doesn't look like the sort of gown one would see you in, Miss Mary," remarked Duke Cravendish.

"No, it's not," said Mary as she examined the gown. She searched through the rest of the packaging until she found a note in the bottom:

To Miss Mary,
I hope you find this gown useful should you change your mind regarding matters we spoke about when we took tea together.
From Madam Boulagise

"Any note from who sent this gown to you?" asked Duke Cravendish.

"Yes, it's been sent on behalf of Madam Boulagise."

"It figures. It has her designer's impression on the gown."

"Well, it's a shame I have no use for such a gown. If you'll forgive me, Duke Cravendish, I need to change for dinner," said Mary as she walked past Duke Cravendish and out of the room.

"Miss Mary, don't you want to take the gown with you?" replied Duke Cravendish to Mary's retreating back.

"Well, it sounds like you know Madam Boulagise's seamstress; you can make sure the gown is returned to her, Duke Cravendish."

"You do know you've got a lady's gown there, Dylan?" said Richard as he entered the library.

"Yes, thank you, Richard. Mary gave it to me and asked me to return it to Madam Boulagise's seamstress. Clearly Madam Boulagise is trying to get to Mary in some way."

"Well, the seamstress will be disappointed to have a gown returned."

"That's why I'm not going to return it. I'm thinking maybe Marinea's seamstress can alter it into something more of Miss Mary's taste."

"I'm sorry to disturb you, Marinea. I was wondering if you could do me a favour?" asked Dylan.

"Of course, Dylan, how can I help you? My, that is a lovely gown, though not to Mary's taste. Although it's lovely material."

"I was hoping you could see if your seamstress could make changes to it to make it more suitable for Miss Mary?"

"Leave it with me, Dylan."

"Though, there is just one more thing, Marinea. Don't mention to Miss Mary where the gown came from."

"You have my word. I won't breathe a word to Mary."

"Thank you for everything. I hope to see you some time in Bristol," said Dylan as he was getting ready to leave the room.

"No doubt you will, Dylan. I wish you all the best, though I hope one day you can see yourself returning to Cattleton. One more thing before you go… don't give up on her, Dylan. She will come around in time."

Chapter Twenty-One

"I'm sorry, Marinea?"

"Mary. She will come around, you just need to give her time."

"Right. Well, thanks. I'll keep that bit of information in mind."

Chapter Twenty-Two

A few days later at the Miller household, Mr and Mrs Miller were sat at the breakfast table when Mary came in to join them.

"Good morning, Marinea, Mr Miller," said Mary.

"Good morning, Mary," said Mr and Mrs Miller.

"If you'll excuse me, ladies, I have some details to sort out with the staff for tomorrow," said Mr Miller as he got up from the table.

Mary noticed the letter in Marinea's hand and just had to ask.

"Is everything alright, Marinea? No bad news from home, I take it?" asked Mary.

"No, not at all, Mary. It just so happens that your mother and my mother seem to have been talking."

"Why do you say that, Marinea?"

"Because Mother's written to me in regards to you staying here and she has made a suggestion about us going somewhere. So, Mr Miller and I thought we could take a trip to Bristol tomorrow and show you the market – and, of course, the harbour, if you are to have any chance of seeing Duke Cravendish," said Marinea cheerfully.

"I take it that part about the harbour was mentioned in your mother's letter," said Mary.

"Yes, it was. I take it that in your letters home, Mary, you never mentioned Duke Cravendish being here."

"No, it would make my mother too happy to know such things."

"So, can I ask you, Mary, are you missing the presence of Duke Cravendish?"

"I suppose it is quieter here now with us being a party of three rather than four."

"Mary, you know that's not what I mean at all. I've seen you in Duke Cravendish's presence; you light up like a debutante entering her first ball."

"Oh no, not you as well, Marinea. Duke Cravendish is charming; he knows it and uses it to his advantage, but he hasn't won me over."

"Yet you said yourself, Mary, that Duke Cravendish has kissed you on more than one occasion, and not just a peck on the cheek."

"He's a born seducer who uses whatever he can to win."

"Well, it appears he still has some work to do with you then, Mary."

"I'm just going to be someone he can't win round."

"Oh, Mary, why won't you open up and let yourself be free with your feelings?"

The following morning at the Miller household, Mary joined Richard and Marinea for breakfast. She was excited about their visit to Bristol that day.

"Good morning, Mary. Are you looking forward to visiting Bristol today? I should warn you that Bristol is a big city and it can be a dangerous place should you end up down the wrong street. Make sure you stay close to Marinea, Mary, for your own safety," said Mr Miller.

"Oh, I intend to, Mr Miller, make no mistake about that. I would hate to run into any pirates."

"Good. The carriage should be here shortly. Have you everything you need?" asked Mr Miller.

Eventually the carriage reached Bristol and Mr Miller tapped his stick against the roof to tell the driver to stop the carriage. Mary had been enjoying the view; she didn't realise they had stopped until Marinea spoke.

"We are here, Mary," said Marinea as Mr Miller was waiting to help her out of the carriage.

"So, this is Bristol. It is certainly a bigger place than I expected it to be and there are so many people here. What's that smell? It doesn't have the city smell I was expecting," said Mary as she took in the sights and smells around her.

"That's the smell of the sea air. Have you never seen the sea or smelt the sea air before, Mary?" asked Mr Miller.

"No, my family have never really left Cattleton; only the odd outing to the Lake District to visit other family members. Father doesn't like being too far away from his farm and land," replied Mary.

"Well, you're in for a real treat then. When we reach the harbour, you'll be able to see all the merchant ships and traders arriving," said Marinea.

"Of course! I forgot, Mr Miller, you have your business in shipping."

"That I do, Mary. I take great interest in what's arriving."

"Come, Mary, let me show you the book stall. They even let women purchase books from them," said Marinea.

"You know me too well, Marinea. Have you been to Bristol a lot of times?"

"Well, Richard and I try to travel down at least once a month, so coming down again this month is no hardship."

"Can I help you there, miss?" asked the stall-holder.

"Oh, I'm just looking, thank you. You have a lot of choice here," replied Mary.

"My, thank you, miss. I like to keep a good stock in for my various customers. I've not seen you here before. Is this your first time here?"

"Yes it is, my first time here in Bristol."

"You're an avid reader, I can tell. So do you have an eye out for anything special? History, maybe? Art? Perhaps plants and herbs are an interesting choice for a young lady?"

"I'll take this and this one please."

"Right you are, miss."

"Mary, watch out!" cried Marinea as a swarm of angry people pushed their way through the market, taking Mary along with them.

"Marinea, Mr Miller!" Mary cried out as she tried to push her way through the angry mob of people. Marinea and Mr Miller were now lost to Mary in the crowd. Oh, how was Mary supposed to find her way back to them? She would head to the harbour as that was where they were going to go to next. No doubt Mary would find them there.

Mary felt like she had been walking for hours and there was still no sign of Marinea or Mr Miller, and the daylight seemed to be fading. The only upside was that the sight of the sea was coming into view, so the harbour wouldn't be far away.

"You alright there, miss, walking on your own in this neighbourhood?"

"I'm alright, just looking for the rest of my party," replied Mary.

"Well, be careful. There are dangerous parts out here for a lady on her own. You never know what could happen."

"Well, thank you for your advice. Hopefully my party is not too far ahead."

"This is not the place for a well-bred lady like yourself. There is an inn not far away; they have rooms in the back for your safety."

"Thank you for the advice, sir."

Then, a few minutes later, another gentleman approached Mary.

"Well, what do we have here? A well-bred woman out on her own," said a different male voice as he grabbed her around the waist.

"What are you doing? Get your hands off me!" shouted Mary.

"Feisty little thing, aren't you? That's alright, I like a little rough myself," said Mary's attacker.

Mary remembered the books she still had and hit her attacker with them. She screamed as the man came back for more, ripping her gown in the process.

"I will show you just how you should treat a man."

"I do believe the lady said no," said Duke Cravendish, who seemed to appear out of nowhere.

"What's it to you, Cravendish? Is she your property?" said Mary's attacker.

"No, she's not. I can assure you she's nobody's property and you should know that no means no."

The vile man stepped away from Mary leaving her stood in the shadows and then Duke Cravendish punched the man who had attacked her.

"If you wanted to have her yourself, Cravendish, you only had to ask."

"Why don't you get out of here, Jack, before I rip you apart? You alright there, miss? You're safe now. I won't harm you."

"Oh, Duke Cravendish, you saved my life, thank you," said Mary, who was probably happy to see Duke Cravendish for only the second time.

"Mary, is that you? What are you doing here, alone in Bristol?" asked Duke Cravendish with concern in his voice.

"I was with Marinea and Mr Miller and we got separated and I was trying to find my way back to them and then that vile man attacked me."

"Shh, it's alright, you're safe now. Your gown is ripped. I have supplies on my ship that I can use to repair your gown so it's suitable. I'm sure I know where Richard and Marinea would go if they were trying to find you. I'll get a messenger to send news round that I've found you and you're alright."

"Why can't you take me back to Mr and Mrs Miller if you know where they are?" asked Mary.

"Believe me, I would, Mary, but this part of the city isn't safe and we could end up running into viler men than Jack."

Chapter Twenty-Three

"So, this is your ship, your pride and joy. But why is it here and not in the harbour?" asked Mary.

"That would be because Skip, my second-in-command, ran the ship into some rocks and we're currently in the process of repairing it. Hence the ship is here and not in its proper docks. Come, Mary, allow me to repair your gown," said Duke Cravendish.

"I don't think it's proper for you to fix it."

"Here, Mary, you can put this on while I fix your gown to make you feel more comfortable."

"How did you get to be so good with a needle and thread, Duke Cravendish?"

"Lots of wounds, being a pirate. You need to stitch up or else you bleed out."

"You've had a run-in with my attacker before, I take it? It seemed personal to you."

"It kind of was, Mary. When I saw Jack attacking you, it reminded me of what happened with my mother. When I was a small boy, my mother and I were having a rare day out together, just the two of us."

"And your mother was attacked."

"Yes, she was attacked, and I was too little to help her and she died there. They killed her right in front of me. I still have nightmares about it happening over and over again. I was plagued by one such nightmare during my time in Bath. My mother was a truly loving woman who saw the best in everybody and thought the streets were safe to walk alone. I'm sorry, I shouldn't have mentioned it; it's just you remind me so much of my mother and seeing you back there had me flashing back to when I was a little boy."

"Oh, Dylan, I'm sorry for your loss, and I'm sorry that brought back painful memories for you."

"It's quite alright, Mary, though I'd prefer it if you didn't mention it to anyone else as it's a private family matter and I would like it to stay that way. Not even Hugh or Richard know the full story. Did you just call me by my given name?"

"I guess I did, didn't I?" said Mary, who was surprised herself that she had used his given name.

"You should make yourself comfortable."

"Why should I do that?"

"Because of what I told you earlier. It's not safe for us to walk back to Richard and Marinea tonight, and if you try to go out on your own, Mary, I will pick you up and carry you back down here. So, like I said, make yourself comfortable."

"Fine then, I will. So did you name your ship after your mother? Eleanor, am I right?"

"Yes, how did you know that?"

"It's just the way you talked about your mother, she clearly meant a great deal to you."

"She did. She was a remarkable woman. You remind me of her in some ways."

"I'm sorry you lost her so early on in your life. Thank you, Dylan, for everything. I want to thank you properly for all you've done for me."

"Mary, there is no need to thank me."

And then Mary did something she never thought she would do. She kissed Dylan. Something had changed. Mary no longer saw him as a rake or a scoundrel; now she saw a man before her who had just opened up the deepest, darkest part of his past to her.

"Mary, it's alright. You don't have to do something you don't want to do," said Dylan as he took a loose curl that had escaped Mary's braid and tucked it behind her ear.

"I want to, Dylan. I could have died tonight and I want to experience the world. Nobody has to know, it would just be between the two of us for just this one night together," said Mary.

"Mary, what is it you want to do for just one night only?" asked Dylan.

"I want to know what it feels like to lay in a man's arms. Please don't tell me your interest in me has faded and I've made a complete fool of myself."

"No, my interest in you has not faded. I'm just concerned if this is truly what you want."

"Oh, Dylan, I've never been more sure of anything in my life."

"Well, in that case…"

Dylan kissed Mary back, letting Mary's gown fall to the floor along with the rest of their clothing.

Dylan woke up the following morning thinking he had just had a wonderful dream, until he turned over on the bed to see Mary sleeping soundly beside him. It wasn't until that moment that Dylan realised that he may have just lost his heart to Miss Mary Barker. After all, he had shared his darkest memory with her last night. Mary looked so peaceful and relaxed as she slept on. He knew he would have to wake her, but he just wanted to hold on to the image of her sleeping for a little while longer.

"Morning, Mary. I need to see you safely back to Marinea and Richard, so I will be above deck if you need anything."

"Thank you, Dylan, for everything you have done for me."

"You're welcome, Mary."

Duke Cravendish was on the deck of his ship when Mary appeared. He was checking to make sure all was clear before escorting Mary off his ship and back to the main area of Bristol, back to the inn where Richard and Marinea were staying.

"Mary, we are pleased to see you back in one piece. It was a relief when we got Dylan's message last night saying he found you," said Richard.

"Mary, we are so pleased that Dylan found you last night. I was so worried for you ever since those people pushed us apart and we got separated," said Marinea.

"Well, I will bid you farewell now, Miss Mary. Take care of yourself now," said Duke Cravendish as he took his leave.

"Goodbye, Duke Cravendish," said Mary.

"The carriage is all ready for us. Are we all ready to return to Bath?" said Mr Miller.

The journey back to Bath didn't seem to take long at all and they were back before they knew it. When they returned, Godfrey was waiting for their arrival and he opened the carriage doors as soon as it had stopped.

"Welcome back Mr and Mrs Miller, Miss Mary," said Godfrey.

"Thank you, Godfrey," said Mr Miller.

"A letter arrived for you earlier today, Miss Mary. It's marked urgent," said Godfrey.

"Thank you, Godfrey," said Mary, taking the letter from him.

"Is everything alright, Mary? You look really pale," asked Marinea.

"It's a letter from Kathleen regarding Linda. Apparently she's further into her pregnancy than she thought and she's been put on bed rest, and mother has requested that I return home as soon as possible. I need to go and pack straight away."

"It's alright, Mary. Richard and I will help sort out transport back to Cattleton for you."

"Of course we will – I'll go arrange a carriage for you now Mary while you get yourself packed," said Mr Miller.

While Mary hurried up the stairs to pack her belongings Marinea rang the bell for one of the household staff.

"You wanted to see me Ma'am?" said Massey, a young member of the household staff.

"Oh, yes Massey you have family up in the north of England do you not?"

Chapter Twenty-Three

"Yes I do Ma'am."

"Oh, good then I wish for you to go and visit them while you accompany my friend back to Cattleton."

"I would be honoured to do so Ma'am."

"Mary, let me introduce you to Massey. She's one of our household staff and she will accompany you on your journey back to Cattleton."

"Oh, Marinea, I couldn't take your staff away from you."

"It's quite alright, Massey's heading up north anyway and she will pass through Cattleton on her journey."

The journey back to Cattleton was a bleak affair compared to her journey to Bath.

"I do apologise to you, Massey, I'm not the best conversationalist at the moment."

"That's quite alright, miss, it's quite understandable in the circumstances. It's quite nice to have a quiet ride. I wish you all the best and I hope everything goes well with your sister's pregnancy."

"Thank you, Massey."

Chapter Twenty-Four

"Mary, you're back finally! I'm sorry I had to drag you back from Bath," said Kathleen.

"It's alright. Kathleen, are you alright? You look worn out," asked Mary with some concern for Kathleen.

"Linda's full of requests and the staff are running around all day tending to her needs. I've been doing what I can, you know; Linda is just so demanding we're all struggling to cope. Of course, Linda was always Mother's favourite so she just lets Linda do what she wants. I know I shouldn't speak badly of Linda, but it's so tiring tending to her needs. I've hardly had any rest," explained Kathleen.

"Oh Mary, it's good to have you back. Linda would like to hear some music, it will help the baby to settle. Linda is not sleeping well with the baby kicking so much. And Mary, play something cheerful, would you? None of that dull stuff you usually play," said Mrs Barker as she entered the room.

"So how did you find your time in Bath, Mary? Was it everything you hoped it would be?" asked Kathleen, eager to hear all about Bath.

"Oh, Kathleen, I'm sure there are more interesting things we could be talking about rather than Mary's time in Bath," said Linda. "Like the fashion trends in Bath. Oh wait, I forgot Mary has no interest in fashion, unless it's in music or books. It has been so quiet around here; we've had no callers of any interest, only Lord Bloom. He has been calling round to see Kathleen. The man's clearly at the Duke's beck and call, arranging the Cravendish estate and everything. Now, if you'll excuse me, I need to get some rest. Run along now," said Linda, dismissing them all from the room.

"Visitor for you, Ma'am. Lord Bloom is here. Shall I send him through?" said Nancy.

"Please do so, Nancy," said Mary.

"Kathleen, good afternoon. I hope you don't mind me calling round again?" said Lord Bloom as he entered the room.

"No, not at all, Lord Bloom," replied Kathleen.

"Hello, Lord Bloom," said Mary.

"Miss Mary, welcome back. How was your time in Bath? Well spent, I hope. Bath seems to have agreed with you, you look wonderful," said Lord Bloom.

"Why, thank you, Lord Bloom. But come, you didn't come here to talk to me."

"I came to check on Kathleen to see how everything was going with Linda," replied Lord Bloom.

"How is everything going for you, Lord Bloom, up at the Cravendish estate? It must be keeping you busy?" asked Mary.

"Well, Lady Beatrice has moved in now and she is helping with the household staff while I'm attending to the grounds staff so all is well."

"Has Lady Beatrice let her house out then?" asked Mary.

"No, not at all. Lady Beatrice has bestowed me the most generous gift of ownership of her house and she has given me her full support in allowing me to settle here in Cattleton permanently; she's even given me her blessing to marry whomever I choose.

"Oh my, that's wonderful news, Lord Bloom to hear that you will be staying in Cattleton. Kathleen has been stuck indoors all day. I am sure she could do with a walk around the grounds, Lord Bloom," suggested Mary.

"Of course, where are my manners? Would you care to join us, Miss Mary?"

"No, I will stay here and keep an eye on Linda. Kathleen is due a break anyway."

"Miss Kathleen, it's a lovely afternoon. How about we take a walk around the orchard together? It's nice to be able to spend time alone with you. I must remember to thank Miss Mary for giving me the opportunity to be with you like this. Kathleen, I was speaking with your father earlier on today and he has given me permission to ask for your hand," said Lord Bloom.

Lord Bloom then dropped down on one knee and took Kathleen's hand in his.

"So, Miss Kathleen Barker, will you do me the honour of becoming my wife and become Lady Kathleen Bloom?" asked Lord Bloom.

"Oh, Lord Bloom, I never thought you would ask. Yes, I'll marry you, Lord Bloom," replied Kathleen, delighted to have finally heard the question she had been waiting for.

"Well then, you've made me the happiest man in the world."

"I hope you don't mind if we have a long engagement Lord Bloom as I would like to have all our family members there."

"I couldn't agree more Kathleen; a year after the day we first met sounds quite fitting to me and I would hate it too if all our family members couldn't be there. I would come back inside but I need to get back to the estate and to thank Lady Beatrice for her support," explained Lord Bloom.

"Where's Kathleen gone? Why are you in here alone? I heard Lord Bloom was here," asked Mrs Barker.

"He is just outside with Kathleen," replied Mary.

"Alone? Well, why are you not outside chaperoning them?"

Kathleen then chose that moment to come back into the room.

"Lord Bloom just proposed to me! I'm going to be Lady Kathleen Bloom! I never thought this day would come and we even have the support of Lady Beatrice," said Kathleen. She couldn't hide the smile on her face.

"Oh my, how wonderful it will be to have a Lord in the family! This calls for a celebration; another daughter engaged to be married. Oh, I must tell Mr Barker straight away! Such wonderful news indeed. It would be even more wonderful news should we hear of Mary getting engaged; I hope it won't be too long. Of course, we must make sure the engagement is known to the rest of Cattleton as soon as possible. And to have Lady Beatrice's support in the matter is high praise indeed. Has Lord Bloom informed his family of your engagement? I wonder how they feel about it," said Mrs Barker, who couldn't stop talking.

"Well, we have both decided that having a long

engagement is best so that all of our relatives can be present for the wedding," said Kathleen.

"That sounds lovely, Kathleen," said Mary.

"Nonsense. Have you heard of anything more ridiculous than a long engagement? Mr Barker, what do you have to say on the matter?" said Mrs Barker.

"If it's what they both want, my dear, who am I to speed up the process?" said Mr Barker.

"Mr Barker, you're the girl's father; it's your job to see this wedding happens quickly, before Lord Bloom can change his mind."

"Lord Bloom's a sensible man, my dear. His head's not easily turned by other people's views. I'm sure it won't be long until Duke Cravendish returns anyway, what with his closest friend getting engaged. He will surely be thinking of getting engaged himself," said Mr Barker, knowing exactly what to say to change the conversation.

"Of course, you're right. I can't wait for Duke Cravendish to return. He's been gone for far too long for my liking. The sooner he returns, the better, that's what I say. Hopefully, when he returns, we will see him get engaged before we know it."

Chapter Twenty-Five

Back in Bristol, on Duke Cravendish's ship, Duke Cravendish and Mr Miller were talking.

"So how's Miss Mary doing? Still keeping Marinea busy?" asked Dylan.

"Miss Mary had to rush back to Cattleton to deal with her youngest sister's pregnancy, or something like that. Why such interest in Miss Mary?" asked Richard.

"Just wondering how's she doing after the ordeal that she went through here in Bristol."

"Hmmm."

"What's that mean, Richard?"

"It's just something Marinea said about you and Mary. I thought she was wrong but now I think she might have a point."

"A point about what?"

"The two of you being good for one another. Anyway, how's the ship looking?" asked Richard.

"As good as new now, which is good because I'm going to sell her and do what my uncle wanted me to do."

"So you're going to focus on making a go of this title then?"

"I sure am. I've already written to my Aunt Beatrice to let her know that I'm serious about living up to my responsibilities."

"Oh, I couldn't be happier for you, Dylan. I'm sure Marinea will feel the same way once I tell her your news."

Back in Cattleton, Mary was off to visit Lady Beatrice.

"Mary, I'm pleased you could make the time to come and see me here," said Lady Beatrice as Mary entered the room.

"It's the least I could do, Lady Beatrice, after all that you are doing for my sister and Lord Bloom," said Mary.

"Think nothing of it, Mary. I've come to think of Lord Bloom as another nephew. Come, I want to hear all about your time in Bath. You are looking extremely well; Bath clearly agreed with you."

"Oh yes, Bath is an absolutely beautiful place. Mr and Mrs Miller took me on an outing to the theatre to see an opera – *The Magic Flute*."

"My, it sounds like you had a wonderful time. I'm pleased we didn't lose you to Bath."

"Oh, that could never happen, Lady Beatrice. Bath was lovely but Cattleton remains my true home. I'm a country girl through and through."

"I'm pleased to hear it, Mary. Would you like some more tea or do you have to rush back to Linda?"

"That would be nice, and then I really should get back."

"Miss Mary, a package came for you when you were out. I left it on the side table for you," said Nancy.

"Thank you, Nancy," replied Mary.

Mary spotted Linda hovering around the parcel.

There was no note with the package, which was strange. Mary unwrapped the package to discover the two books she had purchased in Bristol.

Mary thought to herself that Marinea must have sent them on.

"I must have forgotten these when I was rushing to pack to come back to Cattleton."

"Oh, books. What a boring package to receive. I should have just stayed in bed," said Linda.

"Linda, you shouldn't be so nosy. And you were told to stay in bed for your own good," said Mary.

"Well, I've learned nothing from your package anyway. I was looking to see who had sent it to you. Won't you share who it was that sent it to you?"

"How should I know, Linda? After all, like you said, there is no note or letter attached to the parcel."

However, Mary suspected it could be Marinea who had found them and realised they were Mary's and quickly sent them off in a hurry, forgetting to attach a note. Mary wrote a letter thanking Marinea for returning her books, only to get a reply from Marinea a week later saying she knew nothing about any books. Which left Mary with only one other person who it could be from: Duke Cravendish. But why hadn't he attached a note? Not that Mary was complaining after hearing Linda had been looking around for a note. However, it wasn't until Mary opened up her book on herbs and plants that a note fell out of the cover.

Dear Mary,
I found these on my ship when you left and

*thought it would be a good idea to return them
to their rightful owner. I heard from Richard
that you had to leave Bath in a hurry. I hope
everything is alright.*

From Dylan

After that the summer months seemed to fly by, what
with a small engagement party for Kathleen and Lord
Bloom and preparing for Linda's baby to arrive, that Mary
barely had time to visit Lady Beatrice. It had been such a
long time since her last visit.

"Mary, it's good to see you again. Has Linda had her
baby yet?" asked Lady Beatrice.

"Not yet, Lady Beatrice, it's due in the next week or
two. So how are you, Lady Beatrice?" asked Mary.

"I'm wonderful, Mary. I just received a letter from
Dylan. It's taken a long time to get here though."

"What did Duke Cravendish have to say, Lady Beatrice?"
asked Mary, trying not to show too much interest.

"He's returning to Cattleton in the next couple of
weeks after everything's been dealt with in Bristol and he's
sold his ship."

"So, he's truly going to be focused on doing his duty by
his title. My, that's wonderful news for you, Lady Beatrice."

"Yes, it is. I'm sure it won't be too long before we hear
of Dylan announcing his own engagement."

"Oh. What makes you think that, Lady Beatrice?"

"Dylan loves his ship; he wouldn't give it up for just
anyone. She must be a special young lady indeed."

"Have you any idea who the young lady in question is?"

"I've no idea. Dylan's not mentioned any names, but she's clearly someone special."

"Well, I look forward to hearing the news when it's official. I should get going before Linda tries to get out of bed and wander off because she's bored."

"Of course. I hope to see you again soon, Mary."

Mary just got home in time to hear the sound of Linda crying out. Mary rushed upstairs to see Linda on the bedroom floor.

"I was starved of company and I wanted to hear what was going on downstairs when I fell down and this pain started," said Linda.

"Alright, Linda, let's get you back in bed. The baby is coming, that's what is causing your pain," explained Mary.

"Well, it will have to wait. It's not due for at least another week."

"Well, I'm sorry to disappoint you, but babies come when they're ready Linda," said Mary.

"Why are you still here, Mary? Go and fetch the midwife! I'm not delivering this baby without proper midwife support."

"Mother, Kathleen, can you come in here? Linda's gone into labour," shouted Mary.

"My baby is having her very own baby," said Mrs Barker.

"Yes, Mother. We need hot water and clean towels," said Mary.

"No, Mary, I already told you I want the midwife," said Linda.

"Yes, I know, and I'm telling you, Linda, that you've

got me, Mother and Kathleen here and we will help deliver your baby as the midwife is away elsewhere."

"Don't worry, I know what I'm doing. I've helped deliver both of Jane and Elizabeth's children."

Sixteen hours of intense labour later, Linda finally gave birth to a baby girl. Ellie Rose Thorpe made her presence into the world known with the loudest set of lungs Mary had ever heard. Linda collapsed onto the bed, exhausted.

Mary wrapped up baby Ellie Rose in a towel and Kathleen took her from Mary's hands.

"She is a beautiful little girl, is she not?" said Kathleen.

There was a commotion downstairs. *Whatever is going on down here?* thought Mary as she came downstairs to see Mr Thorpe making his presence known in the house.

"Mr Thorpe, it's nice to see you again," said Mary as she came down the stairs.

"I take it Linda is here?" asked Mr Thorpe.

"Yes, she's upstairs, resting. The birth took a lot out of her. May I offer my congratulations to you, Mr Thorpe. You're now a father to a little girl."

"Look, I bet you're wondering why I'm just turning up here now, and so furious, but I returned home to Brighton after being on assignment to discover that Linda was gone. She'd just left, no note, just vanished."

"I'm sorry, Mr Thorpe, for my sister's reckless behaviour."

Linda was bored on her own in Brighton and had decided to come back home. Clearly marriage wasn't how Linda envisioned things to be, but it was obvious that Mr Thorpe loved Linda, no matter how selfish she could be.

Chapter Twenty-Five

"Would you care to come and see your daughter?" asked Mary.

"I would very much like that, Mary."

"I hope you're alright staying here for a few days until Linda and Ellie Rose are ready to travel."

"Thank you, that would be good of you. I'm on leave from the military for a week so we have no need to rush back to Brighton."

"Well, here we are. Kathleen, will you let Mr Thorpe hold his daughter?"

"Mr Thorpe, let us introduce you to Ellie Rose."

"She is certainly a beautiful little girl. How is Linda doing? Do you think she will be up for seeing me yet?"

"Linda, I do hope you're going to have baby Ellie Rose christened here before you head back to Brighton," said Mrs Barker.

"Of course we are, Mama. In fact, I'll put Mary in charge of arranging it all," said Linda.

"Oh, Mary, there you are. Mama and I have been talking and we thought you could arrange the christening with the church, speak with Father James and all that. You were always close friends as children."

"Of course, Linda," replied Mary.

"Splendid, Mary. We were thinking we could have it on Wednesday."

"Wednesday as in next week?"

"No, this Wednesday."

"You want me to arrange a christening for three days' time?"

"Yes. I'm sure you'll be able to talk Father James around and he'll allow us to have it then."

Chapter Twenty-Six

The next day, Mary set off early to Cattleton Church to see Father James about arranging the christening.

"Miss Mary, it's good to see you again. It's been a while since I've seen you at all, even longer since I've seen you in church," said Father James.

"Sorry James, it's been a busy time," replied Mary.

"Of course, you went away to Bath and then Linda arrived and then she had the baby. You do look well though, Mary, even brighter than normal."

"Oh, thank you, James."

"Are you here for confession? Because I can always make time for you," asked Father James.

"No. However, I've come to see you on behalf of Linda."

"Of course, to have the christening, I see. When are they thinking of having it?"

"Wednesday this week."

"Mary, that's in three days' time!" exclaimed Father James.

"I know, but that's what Linda wants. You know Linda doesn't like to wait for things."

"Look, the best I can do on Wednesday at such short notice is first thing in the morning."

"Oh, thank you, James. I can't thank you enough."

"Mary, may I ask something of you?"

"Of course, James, ask me anything."

"Well, I've been given the opportunity to have my own parish from the end of next month, but the thing is, I need to have a wife."

"I see. So you need me to help find you a suitable young female to become your wife?"

"Actually, Mary, I was hoping you would do me the honour of becoming my wife."

"Oh, James, you're one of my oldest and closest friends and I think it's best we stay that way."

"Oh, so it's not because you've fallen for a gentleman that you met in Bath?"

"What would make you think that, James?"

"It's just that I've never seen you look so happy before. I thought maybe you had found your soulmate."

"Enough talk about me, James. How about Miss Eloise Pinkerton? I know she's always taken a liking to you and she's comfortable enough to marry a gentleman for love."

"Are you sure, Mary, that she would consider marrying a man of the church?"

"I'm definitely sure about it. How about you call around this afternoon and see her? So where is this new parish of yours going to be?"

"It's in Rigsby, so it's still in the county, not too far away."

"Well, we're all going to miss you when you go."

"Thanks, Mary. I'll get the church ready for the christening on Wednesday."

"Thanks, James, I knew I could count on you. All the best with Eloise. I know you two will make such a lovely couple."

"Thanks again, Mary. I just hope you're right. Though I think *I* might be right in regards to there being someone out there for you."

"Goodbye, James. We will see you first thing on Wednesday morning."

"Everything's sorted for Wednesday. Father James can do the christening first thing in the morning," said Mary as she entered the room that Mrs Barker and Linda were in.

"Can he not fit it in later in the day?" asked Linda.

"No, Linda, that's the best he could do at such short notice," replied Mary, amazed that Linda thought that would be possible.

"Hmmm, I was expecting more from you, Mary. Well, you can sort Ellie Rose out on Wednesday morning then as I won't have time."

It was late Tuesday night and Duke Cravendish was just arriving back in Cattleton.

"Oh, Dylan, you're back at last," said Lady Beatrice.

"Aunt Beatrice, what are you doing up so late?" asked Dylan. He had just walked in and wasn't expecting anybody else to be about.

"Waiting to make sure you actually came back."

"Is Hugh waiting up as well?"

"No, he went to bed hours ago. Now that you're here, we have a christening to go to in the morning for the new arrival in the Barker family."

Chapter Twenty-Six

"How am I to be in attendance at a christening when nobody knows I'm here?"

"Well, I might have mentioned to Mrs Barker that you would be back to attend. Do you know, she was most excited to hear that you were due to return today?"

"As well as the rest of Cattleton, I presume."

"Well, we are just a village, after all. News does spread quickly."

Chapter Twenty-Seven

Wednesday morning soon arrived and the christening was going to be a small affair as none of the other family members could make it due to the short notice. Luckily, Lord Bloom and Lady Beatrice were going to be in attendance, as well as a few other residents of Cattleton. Of course, Miss Eloise and her family would also be there to support James, as she had accepted his marriage proposal.

Ellie Rose Thorpe was wearing the christening gown that each member of the Barker family had worn for generations when they were christened. Mary had been up since six o'clock sorting Ellie Rose out.

The church had family members on one side and the rest of the residents of Cattleton on the other.

"What a lovely service, Father James, and thank you for arranging it at short notice. Nothing beats a small gathering of family and friends, and Linda knew I had my heart set on Ellie Rose being christened here. Linda, Rupert and Ellie Rose will be leaving soon to return back to Brighton," said Mrs Barker.

"I only did the service; the rest was down to Mary," said Father James.

Then another resident of Cattleton approached Mrs Barker: a Mrs Marshall who was one of the local village gossips.

"Lovely christening, and Ellie Rose is such a beautiful name. Did you have to go through a lot of trouble arranging everything, Mrs Barker?" asked Mrs Marshall.

"Oh, it was not too much trouble. You know me, anything for my girls, Mrs Marshall," said Mrs Barker.

"Thank you for coming. I do hope you liked the christening. Of course, it means a lot to Linda that you could make it," said Mrs Barker whenever anyone left the church.

"Lady Beatrice, thank you for coming," said Mary.

"Not at all. It's nice to see you again, Mary. You've clearly been busy," said Lady Beatrice who wasn't expecting a reply as Mary's focus was diverted elsewhere.

"Oh, Duke Cravendish, I didn't know you were back in town," said Mary as she saw Duke Cravendish approaching her.

"Well, I only arrived back in Cattleton late last night," replied Duke Cravendish.

"Well, I thank you for coming all the same," said Mary.

"It was my pleasure, Mary."

"There is a small spread put on back at the house for anybody who wishes to partake in a bite to eat."

"So, where were we, Father James, before we got interrupted earlier? We were discussing Mary, I do believe," said Mrs Barker.

"Yes, Mrs Barker. I have a lot to thank Mary for. She

showed me the light when I asked her to marry me; she pointed me in the right direction to Miss Eloise and we both couldn't be happier. I'm sure Mary has given her heart to another gentleman, someone she met in Bath, though she was very secretive about it. Miss Eloise Pinkerton and I are to marry by the end of the month and then at the end of next month, we head to my new parish," said Father James.

"I see. Well, I thank you, Father James, for everything and I hope everything works out for you."

It wasn't until everyone had gone and the Thorpe family had left to return to Brighton that Mrs Barker let her feelings be known.

"Well, I must say, Mary, I had an interesting conversation with Father James after the service. Do you know what he told me?"

"I'm pretty sure I can guess, Mother."

"Mr Barker, were you aware that Father James offered marriage to Mary and she rejected his offer, and even helped him find someone else?"

"Mrs Barker, I've always wanted the best for our children, and if Mary couldn't see herself happily married to Father James, then I accept her decision on the matter."

"Thank you, Father," said Mary.

"However, should Mary find someone she wants to marry, then she will have my blessing in the matter. I've always supported my children to have freedom and independence to follow their dreams and their hearts," said Mr Barker.

"Oh, Mr Barker, you are no help at all," said Mrs Barker.

A few days later Mary is visiting Lady Beatrice again to catch up as they didn't get to talk much at the christening.

"Mary, it's good to see you. Won't you come through? Dylan's just made an extremely expensive purchase. He's had it hidden in the music room, thinking that I will not notice. I don't know who he's trying to fool; nothing gets past me. Have a look for yourself, Mary. It's hidden under that cover over there by the window," said Lady Beatrice.

Mary lifted up the cover to have a look at the purchase.

"Oh my! It's impressive. I've heard of the maker of this piano but I've never seen one before," said Mary.

"Dylan doesn't play, even though I would have liked him to. Clearly the young lady he has taken an interest in must be a lover of playing such a piano," said Lady Beatrice.

"She must be. Should we really be in here if Duke Cravendish has stowed such a gift here for his betrothed?"

"Come then, let us return to the drawing room and I'll ring for some tea. You must inform your sister that my house repairs are coming on well, and should Kathleen and Lord Bloom want to move the date of their wedding, they can do so. The house will be fully restored in the next month or two."

"I will let her know, Lady Beatrice."

"You know, Dylan has asked me to arrange a big engagement party for Lord Bloom and Kathleen here at the estate so all of Hugh's family and friends can be in attendance and I will be able to show off the Cravendish estate in its full glory. Though I am sure it's just an excuse for Dylan to announce his own engagement at the end of the night."

"Really? And do you have any idea who the young lady

in question could be, Lady Beatrice?" asked Mary with some curiosity.

"No, I'm still trying to work that out."

Then Dylan walked into the room carrying his shirt over his shoulder.

"Dylan, you are not on your ship now. You need to make sure you are dressed properly for every occasion. Sort yourself out, we've got company here," said Lady Beatrice sharply.

"I'm sorry to disappoint you, Aunt Beatrice," replied Dylan. "Miss Mary, I didn't know you were here."

"That's quite alright, Duke Cravendish. I was hoping to see you anyway, for my father. May we discuss it privately in your study?" asked Mary.

"Of course, come through," said Duke Cravendish as he leads Mary into his study.

"Is everything alright? Usually your father just sends a messenger over."

"Oh yes, everything's fine. I just wanted to thank you for returning my books to me. It means a lot to me, so thank you. Though I thought Marinea had sent them originally."

"And what's the message from your father?"

"Oh, he hopes that the staff are working out, and if you should require any more assistance then you know where to find him."

"Well, thank him for me, but Lord Bloom's looking after the running of estates for me."

"Oh, I see. Well, could you pass the message on to Lord Bloom then?"

"I'm sure I can manage that. And Mary…"

"Yes?"

Chapter Twenty-Seven

"I heard you turned down Father James's offer of marriage as well."

"Yes. News does travel fast around here in the country; nothing stays quiet for long. If you will excuse me, Duke Cravendish, I need to get back."

"Was that all you wanted to tell me?"

"Yes, that is everything."

Though Mary was actually thinking, *I can't stop thinking about what happened between us on your ship and was thinking you might feel the same. But from just talking to your aunt now, I believe you don't feel the same, as you are soon going to be engaged to someone else.*

"Right, well, I better let you go. I'll pass the message on to Hugh. And, Mary, I look forward to seeing you at Lord Bloom and Kathleen's engagement party."

Why had he just said that? What he actually wanted to say was, *I can't stop thinking about us and our time together on my ship, and I would really like to kiss you again if only you would give me a sign.*

Chapter Twenty-Eight

The day was finally here. Kathleen and Lord Bloom's engagement party was being held at the Cravendish estate.

"Oh, Kathleen, you look wonderful as always," said Mary.

"I'm so nervous about finally meeting Lord Bloom's family. I'm wondering if they're going to like me," said Kathleen.

"Oh, Kathleen, they are going to love you."

"I must say, Mary, you look wonderful as well. I don't believe I've seen that gown before. It's not in your usual style."

"It's something Marinea chose for me when I was in Bath and she sent it to me recently."

"Are you ready to go, girls? Oh my, Mary," gasped Mrs Barker, who was impressed with Mary's choice of gown.

"I know you disapprove of my gown, Mother," said Mary.

"No, not at all this time. This gown is lovely. Are you hoping to see if the gentleman who you met in Bath is there tonight? You want to impress him," said Mrs Barker.

"What gentleman in Bath? Mary, you kept that quiet," said Kathleen, concerned she had missed out on some news.

"I'm sorry to disappoint you both, but there is no gentleman from Bath," replied Mary.

"Well, that's strange. Father James was under the impression that there was a gentleman who had captured your heart in Bath," said Mrs Barker.

At the Cravendish estate, the engagement party was getting well under way and the Barkers had just arrived.

"Oh, Mary, I believe that's Lord Bloom's mother and sister over there. Oh, do wish me luck as I go and introduce myself to them," said Kathleen nervously.

"You'll be fine, Kathleen. I'm sure they will like you very much. After all, seeing Hugh happy will make them happy, right?" said Mary.

"Excuse me, everybody. Good evening to you all. I would like to propose a toast. As you all know, we are here tonight to celebrate the engagement of Hugh Bloom and Kathleen Barker, who met here in this little village of Cattleton. I would like everyone to raise their glasses for the happy couple," said Duke Cravendish.

"For Kathleen and Hugh," everyone cheered out.

"Marinea, Mr Miller, it's good to see you again. There are quite a lot of people here, are there not? Are you staying here at the estate?" enquired Mary.

"Yes, we are. Dylan's repaying the favour after his stay in Bath. I see there are some old faces here who I would like to introduce Richard to. Will you excuse us, Mary?" said Marinea.

"Of course, by all means, Marinea. I'll see you later, I'm sure."

There were a lot of unfamiliar faces here, but one face

was very familiar and not in a good way: Miss Helena Valentine. Mary hadn't seen Helena since the first time she had met Duke Cravendish, back at the beginning of spring in Lord and Lady Peacock's library. Was Duke Cravendish going to announce his engagement to Helena Valentine tonight? Helena was now making her way over to Mary.

"I must congratulate your sister on her engagement. Your sisters do seem to make marrying well an art form. Though your mother won't have the same luck with you, as no man would want you, Mary," said Helena Valentine.

"Thank you, Helena. However, I'm still waiting to hear of your own engagement being announced, or have you not found a gentleman who's willing to have you for more than one night?" replied Mary.

"My, haven't you changed, Mary, speaking to me that way? You just wait. I will be engaged before you know it," retorted Helena Valentine.

"So, have you got someone lined up to propose to you?"

"Come now, you must know, Mary, that Duke Cravendish rushed back to Cattleton and recently brought a piano, which is clearly meant for me as everyone knows I'm the best piano player in all of Cattleton. Now all I have to do is wait for him to ask me. I'm sure I won't have to wait too long. After all, he is on a countdown to marry or he will lose his title to his younger brother. My family know everything about everything you know. A quick wedding will surely be likely," said Helena Valentine gleefully.

Mary felt Duke Cravendish's eyes on her, watching her every move, all evening. Surely a soon-to-be-engaged man should only have eyes for his betrothed? Of course,

Mary had been following Duke Cravendish with her eyes as well, and when she noticed him slip away to his study, she followed him.

"What are you playing at, Duke Cravendish?" asked Mary as she followed Duke Cravendish into his study.

"Mary, come in. What can I do for you?" asked Duke Cravendish.

"Why have you been looking at me all evening when you are soon to be engaged to Helena Valentine?"

"Well, I must say, that's news to me," replied Duke Cravendish in shock.

"You are not getting engaged then?" asked Mary, who was relieved to hear that what Helena had said wasn't true.

"No, I'm not, especially not to Helena Valentine."

"But she knew about your purchase of a new piano."

"Yes she did, because she was in the store when I placed my order for the piano."

"And she also said you rushed back to Cattleton."

"Mary, if you would allow me to get a word in, you seem relieved to hear that I'm not engaged and you seem to take a great deal of interest in my life decisions."

"It's none of my concern what you do. It's just that Lady Beatrice mentioned your recent new purchase of that piano in your music room as well, and you selling your ship when I know it's the love of your life, and how you were settling down here in Cattleton. Then, when I thanked you for returning my books to me, you were so normal, you acted as though nothing had happened between us, and I thought you thought of me as just another conquest, yet I wanted more from you, I wanted you to give me a sign that it wasn't just one-sided and that you were just as affected by what happened between us as I was," said Mary, blurting everything out at once.

"Mary, I could never think of you as just a conquest. I want to ask you something."

"Ask me something? What do you want to ask me?"

"Mary Barker, will you remain your free, adventurous, independent self during the day but share your evenings with me?"

"Duke Cravendish, what are you asking me? Are you asking me what I think you're asking me?"

"No, I couldn't ask that of you after you have turned down two men already. I wouldn't want to be the third man to get my heart broken over you. After all, I lost my heart to you that night we spent together on my ship in Bristol."

"Oh, Dylan, I think I'm in love with you too. When I thought you were going to announce your own engagement here tonight, my heart broke a little inside. I never thought it was possible for me to fall in love, but I believe I'm in love now. With you, that is."

"So what does that mean, Mary?"

"If you were to ask me the question, Duke Cravendish, then I would say yes."

"Well then, would you, Miss Mary Barker, do me the honour of becoming Duchess Cravendish?"

"I will, Dylan Cravendish."

"Of course, I will see your father tomorrow and ask him for your hand in the traditional way. But first, Mary, shall we seal the deal with a kiss?"

Before Mary could answer, Duke Cravendish had embraced Mary in a kiss full of love and tenderness.

Chapter Twenty-Eight

"I don't know what William's going to say when he hears the news."

"Well, that's one way to break the mood, Mary."

"Has me mentioning William's name affected you now?"

"Mary, you shouldn't tease me with such words. We should return back to the ballroom before anybody realises. We are both missing. But surely one more kiss won't hurt."

"I'm afraid it will."

"You're worried I will ravish you senseless then, Mary."

"I know you will if I give you the chance."

"Is that so?"

"Dylan, I…"

Mary felt herself melting as Duke Cravendish kissed her again.

"By the way, I love what Marinea's seamstress did to the gown you're wearing."

"What do you mean, Duke Cravendish?" Mary asked whilst composing herself after Duke Cravendish's kiss.

"It's the same dress Madam Boulagise sent you. I got Marinea to get her seamstress to make alterations to it so it would be more your style."

"Oh, I see. I didn't notice or even think of that when I was getting ready for this evening, though I did want to look my best to show you what you were missing."

Chapter Twenty-Nine

The following morning at the breakfast table in the Barker household, Mrs Barker heard voices in the hallway.

"Well, what's Duke Cravendish doing here so early in the morning? Doesn't he know he's got guests at the Cravendish estate to take care of?" said Mrs Barker as she joined Kathleen in the hallway.

"I don't know, Mother, I only saw Duke Cravendish arrive and head into the study with father," replied Kathleen.

"My, Duke Cravendish, I wasn't expecting to have a caller so early in the morning," said Mr Barker as he showed Duke Cravendish into his study.

"I'm sorry if I disturbed you so early, Mr Barker," said Duke Cravendish.

"No, not at all, Duke Cravendish. I'm always up at the crack of dawn attending to the animals, and besides, morning calls are better as Mrs Barker's less likely to be eavesdropping at the door. So tell me, Duke Cravendish, what can I do for you on this fine morning that could not wait? After all, you've left your guests unattended at the Cravendish estate," said Mr Barker.

"My Aunt Beatrice is there to handle things for me," replied Duke Cravendish.

"I see," said Mr Barker.

"Mr Barker, I have come here this morning to ask for your permission – or, more accurately, your blessing – to have Miss Mary's hand in marriage."

"I see. And have you spoken to Mary regarding this plan of yours? Because I can't give my blessing to such a marriage unless I know it's what she really wants. If you wouldn't mind waiting here, Duke Cravendish," said Mr Barker.

"My, my, people outside my study. Fancy that," said Mr Barker as he opened the study door.

"We are just curious, my dear, about why Duke Cravendish is here?" enquired Mrs Barker.

"I'm sure all will become clear in good time, my dear. Mary, won't you come in here a moment? There are things we need to discuss."

"Of course, Father," said Mary.

"Now, Mary, do you know why I've called you in here?" asked Mr Barker.

"I do."

"Is it true that you have consented to marry Duke Cravendish?"

"I have, Father. I'm in love with Duke Cravendish and he's in love with me, and we hope that you will give us your blessing."

"Of course I will, if that's truly what you desire."

"Thank you, Father," said Mary with some relief.

"Now, who's going to break the good news to your mother?" said Mr Barker.

When Mr Barker finally opened the door to his study, Mrs Barker was the first one to speak.

"Well, is someone going to tell me what's going on here? First Duke Cravendish turns up here at first light, then you call Mary into the study. Am I not to know what's going on in my own household?" said Mrs Barker.

"Well, Mother, we have some good news for you," said Mary.

"Oh, really, my dear? What is this so-called good news?"

"Duke Cravendish and I are now engaged to be married."

"Oh my, Mary, that's wonderful news! Indeed, haven't I always said, Mr Barker, that our Mary was born to be a Duchess?" said Mrs Barker, delighted to hear such news.

"Come, Kathleen, grab your shawl. We must hurry to town and inform everybody of our wonderful news. I can't wait to tell Caroline Valentine the good news. She's always thought her family was better than mine. Well, we will show her otherwise," said Mrs Barker. She couldn't be happier.

"You had better hurry back home before your Aunt Beatrice hears the news from anyone else," said Mr Barker.

"Thank you again, Mr Barker, for everything."

"Just promise me you will take care of her."

"I will, Mr Barker."

"I should go back with you and we can tell Lady Beatrice together," said Mary.

At the Cravendish estate, Lady Beatrice was just coming out of the dining room when Dylan returned.

"Dylan, is it true that you were out this morning before I had even awoken? The staff told me you had gone out," said Lady Beatrice.

"Yes, Aunt Beatrice, and I've brought someone back with me."

"Mary, come on in with you. My, you are here early."

"Lady Beatrice, we have some news to tell you," said Mary.

"Mary and I are engaged to be married," said Dylan.

"Thank the Lord! It's about time the pair of you got together. I've been waiting for such news for weeks," said Lady Beatrice cheerfully.

"I was visiting Mr Barker this morning and he has given us his blessing to marry," replied Dylan.

"I see. Well, it took you both long enough to get there. I've known you two were right for one another since the first time I saw you together," said Lady Beatrice.

"You have? But you never mentioned anything to either of us," Duke Cravendish and Mary said at the same time.

"Enough talk for now. How about the two of you head into the drawing room and I'll see everyone else off," instructed Lady Beatrice.

A few moments later, Lord Bloom and Mr and Mrs Miller came into the room. Marinea rushed over to Mary while Richard and Hugh patted Dylan on the back.

"Oh my, Mary, I'm so happy for you both! Ever since you left Bath, I've longed to hear news of your engagement. I told Dylan not to give up on you and it looks like he didn't," said Marinea.

"Congratulations, Dylan! You've finally found and won over the perfect woman for you," said Richard.

"So, when's the big day going to be?" asked Hugh.

Lady Beatrice came into the room a few minutes later. Before Dylan could answer Hugh's question, his aunt spoke out.

"I've seen the rest of the guests off and sent word to Father James to call around when he's free. I'm sure Mrs Barker's filling in the rest of Cattleton right now," said Lady Beatrice.

"Father James to see you, Lady Beatrice," said one of the servants.

"Is everything alright? I got an urgent message saying you wanted to see me," asked Father James with concern in his voice.

"Yes, thank you for coming so quickly. I want to ask you to conduct one more wedding before you leave for your new parish. Won't you come through?" said Lady Beatrice.

"Duke Cravendish, it is an honour, though I don't know why you would request my presence?" said Father James, puzzled.

"That would be down to my betrothed. I believe you are old friends," explained Dylan.

"Mary, you and Duke Cravendish are the ones getting married?" asked Father James.

"Yes," replied Mary.

"So when do you want to arrange it for?" asked Father James.

"As soon as possible. This week would be good," said Duke Cravendish.

"This week!" exclaimed Father James.

"Well, Father James, we are all here to help with the arrangements," said Lady Beatrice.

"No, we're only joking. But as soon as possible, before Mary here changes her mind about marrying me," said Duke Cravendish.

"Oh, Dylan, I'm not going to change my mind. Don't be so silly," replied Mary.

Barely a week had gone by and the day was finally here: the wedding of Duke Dylan Cravendish and Miss Mary Barker.

"Congratulations to the pair of you on your blessed day," said Lady Beatrice.

"Four daughters married and one engaged to be married! Oh, Mr Barker, can you think of a more blessed day?" said Mrs Barker.

Nobody would be calling Mary the spinster Barker daughter from now on. As Mary knew, she would now be known as Duchess Cravendish and she couldn't be happier. She had finally found herself and had also found true love.

Chapter Thirty

Six months later, the wedding of Kathleen and Lord Bloom had finally arrived.

"So, are you ready to finally get married?" asked Dylan.

"I can't believe that I'm getting married after you, Dylan. How is Mary finding things as Duchess Cravendish?" asked Hugh.

"She couldn't be happier. She's teaching the children of the tenants to read and teaching some of them how to play the piano, and enjoying being free to do what she wants during the day. I'm soon going to be a father as well, if you can believe that," said Dylan.

"Congratulations! I do believe Kathleen mentioned that you were starting a family."

"Hello, Hugh. I thought it was you. All ready for the big day, are you? Just checking on your best man, making sure he's ready?" said Mary as she entered the room.

"Mary, you're looking well," said Hugh.

"Thank you, Hugh, you're too kind. You know I look like a balloon though," replied Mary.

"Not long left, I take it?"

"Still got a few months to go yet. I can't do anything at the moment without this one hovering over me. I don't know what he will be like when it is time for the little one to arrive."

"I never thought I would see the day Dylan would be fretting over a woman! Though it is good to see you two are both still very much in love."

Later on at the church, most of the guests were beginning to take their seats. Mary spotted Father James and Eloise entering the church.

"Father James, Eloise, it's good to see you again. How's the new parish going?" asked Mary.

"It's all good, Mary. I see you and Eloise are in the same way. How far are you along?" asked Father James.

"About five months. Dylan is always fretting over me, though," said Mary.

"The same, though I think James is fretting less than Dylan," replied Eloise.

"Thanks to the both of you for coming."

"Oh, we wouldn't miss it for the world. James sees the Barker family as his own," said Eloise.

"Oh, here comes your mother. We better take our seats before she stops us all to talk, and then there will be no getting away."

"Oh, isn't it lovely. Everyone is here, William and Edward in matching suits and your sisters with their husbands and children. And Mary, you're getting so big!" said Mrs Barker.

"Yes, thank you, Mother."

"And I see you're sitting on the groom's side."

"Well, Dylan is the best man."

"Of course, you're married now."

"Can everyone take their seats, please?" said the reverend who was going to conduct the service. Kathleen was starting to make her way down the aisle with Mr Barker.

The service went without a hitch.

Then it was time for the wedding breakfast and the Bloom and Barker families were situated on one table.

"Oh, Mr Barker, can you believe it? I never thought I would see the day all five of my daughters were married. Now I just need to focus on finding William a wife," said Mrs Barker.

"Good heavens, woman! Can't you give up match-making now all our five daughters are married?" said Mr Barker.

"I intend to see all my children married before I give up match-making," replied Mrs Barker.

"Well, good luck, William. You're going need it," replied Mary.

"Oh, thanks for that, Mary. I'm pleased to see you're happy and well," said William.

They were all enjoying the reception toasts and speeches had been delivered when Mary suddenly stood up and walked out. Dylan went after her to check she was alright.

"Mary, are all alright?" asked Dylan, concerned about her and the baby.

"I'm fine, I just needed to get some air," replied Mary.

Then Mary suddenly felt like she was going to faint. Dylan caught her before she fell and helped her to sit down.

"Mary, you are not alright. You're not the type of

female to faint. Could there be something wrong with the baby? Do you need me to get Doctor White?"

"No, Dylan, I'm fine. Stop fretting. Oh, maybe I could do with seeing the doctor after all," said Mary as she experienced shooting pains down both sides of her body.

"Let's get you back home and to bed," said Dylan as he dispatched a servant to fetch Doctor White.

"Well, hello Mary," said Doctor White as he came into the bedroom.

"Doctor White," said Mary.

"You sent for me, I believe," said Doctor White.

"Do you think there is something wrong with the baby?" asked Dylan.

"Let's take a little look and a listen, shall we?" said Doctor White.

"Is everything alright, Doctor? She's not going to lose the baby, is she?" asked Dylan.

"No, everything's fine, though I must tell you, I heard two good heartbeats."

"Mary and the baby are doing well, then."

"No, the doctor means we're having twins, Dylan. Right, Doctor White?" asked Mary.

"Yes, that's right, twins. Very unusual. You're only the second patient that I've had having twins."

"So, the pain either side was each twin making themselves comfortable. Please tell him I don't need bed rest."

"Yes, that's correct, and no, she's right, she doesn't need to stay in bed, though she should take it easy. Don't overdo it or I will have to come back here and put you on bed rest. Make sure she does as she's told," said Doctor White.

"Thank you, Doctor. I will show you out," said Dylan.

After Dylan had seen Doctor White out, he returned back to Mary's side.

"See, everything's alright and you're not bigger than you're supposed to be, it's twins. Make sure you don't go overexerting yourself," said Dylan.

"Mary, is everything alright or were you two trying to get away early and using the doctor for cover?" said Lady Beatrice half-jokingly as she entered the room.

"Everything's alright, Lady Beatrice, just a scare. It turns out we're having twins," said Mary.

"Oh my, how wonderful! And Mary, we are family now – it's Aunt Beatrice, not Lady Beatrice. I should have guessed it was twins. Dylan's mother's mother was a twin; you know, they say it runs in families."

"Thanks, we could have done with knowing that sooner, Aunt Beatrice," said Dylan.

Two and a half months later, after finally being put on bed rest less than a week before, Mary went into labour, which seemed to last for days. Dylan had been banished from the room and had taken to pacing outside. He didn't know what he would do if he lost them. Should it be taking so long?

"Hush, Dylan, the babies will make their appearance when they are ready," said Lady Beatrice.

"Thank you, Aunt Beatrice," said Dylan.

Hugh called round with Kathleen to help Dylan take his mind off things.

"Mary's strong, Dylan, and childbirth can take a while, so I've been told. And besides, I'm sure that as it's twins, it will take twice as long," said Hugh.

Mary felt the contractions wash over her. She knew from delivering babies herself that labour could take a while. It was just over an hour later and the cries of the first baby filled the air, then a few minutes later, the second one made its appearance.

"You can come in now, Dylan," said the midwife who had just delivered the babies.

"Hello, is everyone alright in here?" said Dylan as he made his way into the room.

"Dylan, we've got a girl and a boy. I was hoping, if it's alright with you, that we could name them after your family," said Mary.

"Oh, Mary, I couldn't ask for anything more."

"Well then, let me introduce you to Eleanor Cravendish and Hugh Cravendish, after your mother and your best friend."

"Oh, Mary, I couldn't ask for more. Kathleen and Hugh are here, by the way. They are downstairs. They came to check on us."

"Go on, then, let's invite them up and show off Eleanor and Hugh."

"Hello Kathleen, Hugh," said Mary as they entered the room to see Eleanor and Hugh.

"Oh, Mary, it's good to see you're alright! And who are these two?" said Kathleen.

"Let us introduce you to your new namesake. Hugh, meet Hugh Cravendish," said Mary.

"Oh my, that's lovely. What made you call him Hugh?" asked Hugh.

"You're a great gentleman and hopefully a great role model for Hugh here," replied Mary.

"What's your little girl called then, Mary?" asked Kathleen.

"We have named her after Dylan's mother, Eleanor."

"Oh, hello Hugh and Eleanor Cravendish. It's nice to meet you both," said Kathleen.

"Well, I must say, you would have made Oscar proud. If he was here, that is," said Lady Beatrice. "And I'm mighty proud of the pair of you too. Mr Petterson left this note to only be opened once you had created your own family. It's from Oscar; he asked for it to be left until the next generation had arrived. I don't know what it says; it's been sealed since the day Oscar wrote it."

"What does it say, Dylan?"

To my nephew Dylan,

If you are reading this letter you have fulfilled my requirements. I was very much an admirer of your mother Eleanor and I was devastated when I heard of your mother's passing. Eleanor was certainly a wonderful woman who my brother didn't deserve. I had the pleasure of meeting you with your mother when you were just a little boy. I saw a lot of myself in you and Eleanor's spirit in you. I never found anyone to love and settle down with, though I loved you like the son I could never have. I'm truly happy that Eleanor's genes live on in you and your family.

Signed Oscar Cravendish

"Well, that explains a lot; why Oscar left you the title, at least. Your mother's death must have affected Oscar greatly as well, driving him to be a recluse, and he clearly didn't want to see you go the same way," said Lady Beatrice.

"If I hadn't met you, Mary, I could have gone the same way as Oscar."

"I could say the same about you, Dylan. If we hadn't found each other, we could have both gone the same way as Oscar," said Mary.

Acknowledgements

Firstly, I wish to thank my family for supporting me in this endeavour, especially my mum who has been my sounding board and the one to encourage me to go ahead and do this. Secondly, I wish to thank the author Mary Chapman for her advice. Thirdly, I would like to thank all the English teachers I had at school who had to read my first stories when everything was handwritten, and I had terrible handwriting. Last but not least, a big thank you to you, dear reader, for choosing to read *Mary and the Duke*.

About the Author

Daisy grew up in the countryside in Lincolnshire. She is proud to say she is left-handed. Daisy has always had a love for the written word and reading. She is a huge fan of historical romance novels, especially the classics. In her free time, she also enjoys baking and watching romantic movies. When Daisy isn't writing, she can be found working in a hotel in the food and beverage department. *Mary and the Duke* is Daisy's first novel.

 Matador

For exclusive discounts on Matador titles,
sign up to our occasional newsletter at
troubador.co.uk/bookshop